The Entail

By

E. T. A. Hoffmann

British Library Cataloguing-in-Publication Data
A catalogue record for this book is available from the
British Library

E. T. A. Hoffman

Ernst Theodor Wilhelm Hoffmann was born in Königsberg, East Prussia in 1776. His family were all jurists, and during his youth he was initially encouraged to pursue a career in law. However, in his late teens Hoffman became increasingly interested in literature and philosophy, and spent much of his time reading German classicists and attending lectures by, amongst others, Immanuel Kant.

In was in his twenties, upon moving with his uncle to Berlin, that Hoffman first began to promote himself as a composer, writing an operetta called Die Maske and entering a number of playwriting competitions. Hoffman struggled to establish himself anywhere for a while, flitting between a number of cities and dodging the attentions of Napoleon's occupying troops. In 1808, while living in Bamberg, he began his job as a theatre manager and a music critic, and Hoffman's break came a year later, with the publication of Ritter Gluck. The story centred on a man who meets, or thinks he has met, a long-dead composer, and played into the 'doppelgänger' theme – at that time very popular in literature. It was shortly after this that Hoffman began to use the pseudonym E. T. A. Hoffmann, declaring the 'A' to stand for 'Amadeus', as a tribute to the great composer, Mozart.

Over the next decade, while moving between Dresden, Leipzig and Berlin, Hoffman produced a great range of both literary and musical works. Probably Hoffman's most well-known story, produced in 1816, is 'The Nutcracker and the Mouse King', due to the fact that – some seventy-six years later - it inspired Tchaikovsky's ballet The Nutcracker.

In the same vein, his story 'The Sandman' provided both the inspiration for Léo Delibes's ballet Coppélia, and the basis for a highly influential essay by Sigmund Freud, called 'The Uncanny'. (Indeed, Freud referred to Hoffman as the "unrivalled master of the uncanny in literature.")

Alcohol abuse and syphilis eventually took a great toll on Hoffman though, and – having spent the last year of his life paralysed – he died in Berlin in 1822, aged just 46. His legacy is a powerful one, however: He is seen as a pioneer of both Romanticism and fantasy literature, and his novella, Mademoiselle de Scudéri: A Tale from the Times of Louis XIV is often cited as the first ever detective story.

The Entail

Not far from the shore of the Baltic Sea is situated the ancestral castle of the noble family Von R——, called R— sitten. It is a wild and desolate neighbourhood, hardly anything more than a single blade of grass shooting up here and there from the bottomless drift-sand; and instead of the garden that generally ornaments a baronial residence, the bare walls are approached on the landward side by a thin forest of firs, that with their never-changing vesture of gloom despise the bright garniture of Spring, and where, instead of the joyous carolling of little birds awakened anew to gladness, nothing is heard but the ominous croak of the raven and the whirring scream of the storm-boding sea-gull. A quarter of a mile distant Nature suddenly changes. As if by the wave of a magician's wand you are transported into the midst of thriving fields, fertile arable land, and meadows. You see, too, the large and prosperous village, with the land-steward's spacious dwelling-house; and at the angle of a pleasant thicket of alders you may observe the foundations of a large castle, which one of the former proprietors had intended to erect. His successors, however, living on their property in Courland, left the building in its unfinished state; nor would Freiherrl Roderick von R—— proceed with the structure when he again took up his residence on the ancestral estate, since the lonely old castle was more suitable to his temperament, which was morose and averse to human society. He had its ruinous walls repaired as well as circumstances would admit, and then shut himself up within them along with a cross-grained house-steward and a slender establishment of servants.

He was seldom seen in the village, but on the other hand he often walked and rode along the sea-beach; and people claimed to have heard him from a distance, talking to the waves and listening to the rolling and hissing of the surf, as though he could hear the answering voice of the spirit of the sea. Upon the topmost summit of the watch-tower he had a sort of study fitted up and supplied with telescopes — with a complete set of astronomical apparatus, in fact. Thence during the daytime he frequently watched the ships sailing past on the distant horizon like white-winged sea-gulls; and there he spent the starlight nights engaged in astronomical, or, as some professed to know, with astrological labours, in which the old house-steward assisted him. At any rate the rumour was current during his own lifetime that he was devoted to the occult sciences or the so-called Black Art, and that he had been driven out of Courland in consequence of the failure of an experiment by which an august princely house had been most seriously offended. The slightest allusion to his residence in Courland filled him with horror; but for all the troubles which had there unhinged the tenor of his life he held his predecessors entirely to blame, in that they had wickedly deserted the home of their ancestors. In order to fetter, for the future, at least the head of the family to the ancestral castle, he converted it into a property of entail. The sovereign was the more willing to ratify this arrangement since by its means he would secure for his country a family distinguished for all chivalrous virtues, and which had already begun to ramify into foreign countries.

Neither Roderick's son Hubert, nor the next Roderick, who was so called after his grandfather, would live in their ancestral castle; both preferred Courland. It is conceivable, too, that, being more cheerful and fond of life than the gloomy astrologer, they were repelled by the grim loneliness of the place. Freiherr Roderick had granted shelter and subsistence on the property to two old maids, sisters of his father, who were living in indigence, having been but niggardly provided for. They, together with an aged serving-woman, occupied the small warm rooms of one of the wings; besides them and the cook, who had a large apartment on the ground floor adjoining the kitchen, the only other person was a worn-out chasseur, who tottered about through the lofty rooms and halls of the main building, and discharged the duties of castellan. The rest of the servants lived in the village with the land-steward. The only time at which the desolated and deserted castle became the scene of life and activity was late in autumn, when the snow first began to fall and the season for wolf-hunting and boar-hunting arrived. Then came Freiherr Roderick with his wife, attended by relatives and friends and a numerous retinue, from Courland. The neighbouring nobility, and even amateur lovers of the chase who lived in the town hard by, came down in such numbers that the main building, together with the wings, barely sufficed to hold the crowd of guests. Well-served fires roared in all the stoves and fireplaces, while the spits were creaking from early dawn until late at night, and hundreds of light-hearted people, masters and servants, were running up and down stairs; here was heard the jingling and rattling of drinking glasses and jovial hunting choruses, there the footsteps of those dancing to the sound of the shrill music,—everywhere loud mirth and jollity; so that for four or five weeks together the castle was more like a first-rate hostelry situated on a main highroad than the abode of a country gentleman. This time Freiherr Roderick devoted, as well as he was able, to serious business, for, withdrawing from the revelry of his guests, he discharged the duties attached to his position as lord of the entail. He not only had a complete statement of the revenues laid before him, but he listened to every proposal for improvement and to every the least complaint of his tenants, endeavouring to establish order in everything, and check all wrongdoing and injustice as far as lay in his power.

In these matters of business he was honestly assisted by the old advocate V——, who had been law agent of the R—— family and Justitiarius2 of their estates in P—— from father to son for many years; accordingly, V—— was wont to set out for the estate at least a week before the day fixed for the arrival of the Freiherr. In the year 179 — the time came round again when old V—— was to start on his journey for R— sitten. However strong and healthy the old man, now seventy years of age, might feel, he was yet quite assured that a helping hand would prove beneficial to him in his business. So he said to me one day as if in jest, "Cousin!" (I was his great-nephew, but he called me "cousin," owing to the fact that his own Christian name and mine were both the same)—"Cousin, I was thinking it would not be amiss if you went along with me to R— sitten and felt the sea-breezes blow about your ears a bit. Besides giving me good help in my often laborious work, you may for once in a while see how you like the rollicking life of a hunter, and how, after drawing up a neatly-written protocol one morning, you will frame the next when you come to look in the glaring eyes of such a sturdy brute as a grim shaggy wolf or a wild boar gnashing his teeth, and whether you know how to bring him down with a well-aimed shot." Of course I could not have heard such strange accounts of the merry hunting parties at R— sitten, or entertain such a true heartfelt affection for my excellent old great-uncle as I did, without being highly delighted that he wanted to take me with him this time. As I was already pretty well skilled in the sort of business he had to transact, I promised to work with unwearied industry, so as to relieve him of all care and trouble.

Next day we sat in the carriage on our way to R— sitten, well wrapped up in good fur coats, driving through a thick snowstorm, the first harbinger of the coming winter. On the journey the old gentleman told me many remarkable stories about the Freiherr Roderick, who had established the estate-tail and appointed him (V——), in spite of his youth, to be his Justitiarius and executor. He spoke of the harsh and violent character of the old nobleman, which seemed to be inherited by all the family, since even the present master of the estate, whom he had known as a mild-tempered and almost effeminate youth, acquired more and more as the years went by the same disposition. He therefore recommended me strongly to behave with as much resolute self-reliance and as little embarrassment as possible, if I desired to possess any consideration in the Freiherr's eyes; and at length he began to describe the apartments in the castle which he had selected to be his own once for all, since they were warm and comfortable, and so conveniently retired that we could withdraw from the noisy convivialities of the hilarious company whenever we pleased. The rooms, namely, which were on every visit reserved for him, were two small ones, hung with warm tapestry, close beside the large hall of justice, in the wing opposite that in which the two old maids resided.

At last, after a rapid but wearying journey, we arrived at R— sitten, late at night. We drove through the village; it was Sunday, and from the alehouse proceeded the sounds of music, and dancing, and merrymaking; the steward's house was lit up from basement to garret, and music and song were there too. All the more striking therefore was the inhospitable desolation into which we now drove. The sea-wind howled in sharp cutting dirges as it were about us, whilst the sombre firs, as if they had been roused by the wind from a deep magic trance, groaned hoarsely in a responsive chorus. The bare black walls of the castle towered above the snow-covered ground; we drew up at the gates, which were fast

locked. But no shouting or cracking of whips, no knocking
or hammering, was of any avail; the whole castle seemed to
be dead; not a single light was visible at any of the windows.
The old gentleman shouted in his strong stentorian voice,
"Francis, Francis, where the deuce are you? In the devil's
name rouse yourself; we are all freezing here outside the gates.
The snow is cutting our faces till they bleed. Why the devil
don't you stir yourself?" Then the watch-dog began to whine,
and a wandering light was visible on the ground floor. There
was a rattling of keys, and soon the ponderous wings of the
gate creaked back on their hinges. "Ha! a hearty welcome, a
hearty welcome, Herr Justitiarius. Ugh! it's rough weather!"
cried old Francis, holding the lantern above his head, so that
the light fell full upon his withered face, which was drawn up
into a curious grimace, that was meant for a friendly smile.
The carriage drove into the court, and we got out; then I
obtained a full view of the old servant's extraordinary figure,
almost hidden in his wide old-fashioned chasseur livery,
with its many extraordinary lace decorations. Whilst there
were only a few grey locks on his broad white forehead, the
lower part of his face wore the ruddy hue of health; and,
notwithstanding that the cramped muscles of his face gave
it something of the appearance of a whimsical mask, yet the
rather stupid good-nature which beamed from his eyes and
played about his mouth compensated for all the rest.

"Now, old Francis," began my great-uncle, knocking the
snow from his fur coat in the entrance hall, "now, old man,
is everything prepared? Have you had the hangings in my

room well dusted, and the beds carried in? and have you had a big roaring fire both yesterday and today?" "No," replied Francis, quite calmly, "no, my worshipful Herr Justitiarius, we've got none of that done." "Good Heavens!" burst out my great-uncle, "I wrote to you in proper time; you know that I always come at the time I fix. Here's a fine piece of stupid carelessness! I shall have to sleep in rooms as cold as ice." "But you see, worshipful Herr Justitiarius," continued Francis, most carefully clipping a burning thief from the wick of the candle with the snuffers and stamping it out with his foot, "but, you see, sir, all that would not have been of much good, especially the fires, for the wind and the snow have taken up their quarters too much in the rooms, driving in through the broken windows, and then"—— "What!" cried my uncle, interrupting him as he spread out his fur coat and placing his arms akimbo, "do you mean to tell me the windows are broken, and you, the castellan of the house, have done nothing to get them mended?" "But, worshipful Herr Justitiarius," resumed the old servant calmly and composedly, "but we can't very well get at them owing to the great masses of stones and rubbish lying all over the room." "Damn it all, how come there to be stones and rubbish in my room?" cried my uncle. "Your lasting health and good luck, young gentleman!" said the old man, bowing politely to me, as I happened to sneeze;3 but he immediately added, "They are the stones and plaster of the partition wall which fell in at the great shock." "Have you had an earthquake?" blazed up my uncle, now fairly in a rage. "No, not an earthquake,

worshipful Herr Justitiarius," replied the old man, grinning
all over his face, "but three days ago the heavy wainscot
ceiling of the justice-hall fell in with a tremendous crash."
"Then may the"——— My uncle was about to rip out a terrific
oath in his violent passionate manner, but jerking up his
right arm above his head and taking off his fox-skin cap
with his left, he suddenly checked himself; and turning to
me, he said with a hearty laugh, "By my troth, cousin, we
must hold our tongues; we mustn't ask any more questions,
or else we shall hear of some still worse misfortune, or have
the whole castle tumbling to pieces about our ears." "But,"
he continued, wheeling round again to the old servant, "but,
bless me, Francis, could you not have had the common sense
to get me another room cleaned and warmed? Could you
not have quickly fitted up a room in the main building for
the court-day?" "All that has been already done," said the old
man, pointing to the staircase with a gesture that invited us
to follow him, and at once beginning to ascend them. "Now
there's a most curious noodle for you!" exclaimed my uncle
as we followed old Francis. The way led through long lofty
vaulted corridors, in the dense darkness of which Francis's
flickering light threw a strange reflection. The pillars, capitals,
and vari-coloured arches seemed as if they were floating
before us in the air; our own shadows stalked along beside us
in gigantic shape, and the grotesque paintings on the walls
over which they glided seemed all of a tremble and shake;
whilst their voices, we could imagine, were whispering in
the sound of our echoing footsteps, "Wake us not, oh! wake

us not — us whimsical spirits who sleep here in these old stones." At last, after we had traversed a long suite of cold and gloomy apartments, Francis opened the door of a hall in which a fire blazing brightly in the grate offered us as it were a home-like welcome with its pleasant crackling. I felt quite comfortable the moment I entered, but my uncle, standing still in the middle of the hall, looked round him and said in a tone which was so very grave as to be almost solemn, "And so this is to be the justice-hall!" Francis held his candle above his head, so that my eye fell upon a light spot in the wide dark wall about the size of a door; then he said in a pained and muffled voice, "Justice has been already dealt out here." "What possesses you, old man?" asked my uncle, quickly throwing aside his fur coat and drawing near to the fire. "It slipped over my lips, I couldn't help it," said Francis; then he lit the great candles and opened the door of the adjoining room, which was very snugly fitted up for our reception. In a short time a table was spread for us before the fire, and the old man served us with several well-dressed dishes, which were followed by a brimming bowl of punch, prepared in true Northern style,— a very acceptable sight to two weary travellers like my uncle and myself. My uncle then, tired with his journey, went to bed as soon as he had finished supper; but my spirits were too much excited by the novelty and strangeness of the place, as well as by the punch, for me to think of sleep. Meanwhile, Francis cleared the table, stirred up the fire, and bowing and scraping politely, left me to myself.

Now I sat alone in the lofty spacious Rittersaal or Knight's Hall. The snow-flakes had ceased to beat against the lattice, and the storm had ceased to whistle; the sky was clear, and the bright full moon shone in through the wide oriel-windows, illuminating with magical effect all the dark corners of the curious room into which the dim light of my candles and the fire could not penetrate. As one often finds in old castles, the walls and ceiling of the hall were ornamented in a peculiar antique fashion, the former with fantastic paintings and carvings, gilded and coloured in gorgeous tints, the latter with heavy wainscoting. Standing out conspicuously from the great pictures, which represented for the most part wild bloody scenes in bear-hunts and wolf-hunts, were the heads of men and animals carved in wood and joined on to the painted bodies, so that the whole, especially in the flickering light of the fire and the soft beams of the moon, had an effect as if all were alive and instinct with terrible reality. Between these pictures reliefs of knights had been inserted, of life size, walking along in hunting costume; probably they were the ancestors of the family who had delighted in the chase. Everything, both in the paintings and in the carved work, bore the dingy hue of extreme old age; so much the more conspicuous therefore was the bright bare place on that one of the walls through which were two doors leading into adjoining apartments. I soon concluded that there too there must have been a door, that had been bricked up later; and hence it was that this new part of the wall, which had neither been painted like the rest, nor yet ornamented with carvings, formed such a striking contrast with the others. Who does not know with what mysterious power the mind is enthralled in the midst of unusual and singularly strange circumstances? Even the dullest imagination is aroused when it comes into a valley girt around by fantastic rocks, or within the gloomy walls of a church or an abbey, and it begins to have glimpses of things it has never yet experienced. When I add that I was twenty years of age, and had drunk several glasses of strong punch, it will easily be conceived that as I sat thus in the Rittersaal I was in a more exceptional frame of mind than I had ever been before. Let the reader picture to himself the stillness of the night within, and without the rumbling roar of the sea — the peculiar piping of the wind, which rang upon my ears like the tones of a mighty organ played upon by spectral hands — the passing scudding clouds which, shining bright and white, often seemed to peep in through the rattling oriel-windows like giants sailings past — in very truth, I felt, from the slight shudder which shook me, that possibly a new sphere of existences might now be revealed to me visibly and perceptibly. But this feeling was like the shivery sensations that one has on hearing a graphically narrated ghost story, such as we all like. At this moment it occurred to me that I should never be in a more seasonable mood for reading the book which, in common with every one who had the least leaning towards the romantic, I at that time carried about in my pocket,— I mean Schiller's "Ghost-seer." I read and read, and my imagination grew ever more and more excited.

I came to the marvellously enthralling description of the wedding feast at Count Von V——'s.

Just as I was reading of the entrance of Jeronimo's bloody figure,4 the door leading from the gallery into the antechamber flew open with a tremendous bang. I started to my feet in terror; the book fell from my hands. In the very same moment, however, all was still again, and I began to be ashamed of my childish fears. The door must have been burst open by a strong gust of wind or in some other natural manner. It is nothing; my over-strained fancy converts every ordinary occurrence into the supernatural. Having thus calmed my fears, I picked up my book from the ground, and again threw myself in the arm-chair; but there came a sound of soft, slow, measured footsteps moving diagonally across the hall, whilst there was a sighing and moaning at intervals, and in this sighing and moaning there was expressed the deepest trouble, the most hopeless grief, that a human being can know. "Ha! it must be some sick animal locked up somewhere in the basement storey. Such acoustic deceptions at night time, making distant sounds appear close at hand, are well known to everybody. Who will suffer himself to be terrified at such a thing as that?" Thus I calmed my fears again. But now there was a scratching at the new portion of the wall, whilst louder and deeper sighs were audible, as if gasped out by some one in the last throes of mortal anguish. "Yes, yes; it is some poor animal locked up somewhere; I will shout as loudly as I can, I will stamp violently on the floor, then all will be still, or else the animal below will make itself heard more distinctly, and in its natural cries," I thought. But the blood ran cold in my veins; the cold sweat, too, stood upon my forehead, and I remained sitting in my chair as if transfixed, quite unable to rise, still less to cry out. At length the abominable scratching ceased, and I again heard the footsteps. Life and motion seemed to be awakened in me; I leapt to my feet, and went two or three steps forward. But then there came an ice-cold draught of wind through the hall, whilst at the same moment the moon cast her bright light upon the statue of a grave if not almost terrible-looking man; and then, as though his warning voice rang through the louder thunders of the waves and the shriller piping of the wind, I heard distinctly, "No further, no further! or you will sink beneath all the fearful horrors of the world of spectres." Then the door was slammed too with the same violent bang as before, and I plainly heard the footsteps in the anteroom, then going down the stairs. The main door of the castle was opened with a creaking noise, and afterwards closed again. Then it seemed as if a horse were brought out of the stable, and after a while taken back again, and finally all was still.

At that same moment my attention was attracted to my old uncle in the adjoining room; he was groaning and moaning painfully. This brought me fully to consciousness again; I seized the candles and hurried into the room to him. He appeared to be struggling with an ugly, unpleasant dream. "Wake up, wake up!" I cried loudly, taking him gently by the hand, and letting the full glare of the light fall upon his face. He started up with a stifled shout, and then, looking kindly at me, said, "Ay, you have done quite right — that you have, cousin, to wake me. I have had a very ugly dream, and it's all solely owing to this room and that hall, for they made me think of past times and many wonderful things that have happened here. But now let us turn to and have a good sound sleep." Therewith the old gentleman rolled himself in the bed-covering and appeared to fall asleep at once. But when I had extinguished the candles and likewise crept into bed, I heard him praying in a low tone to himself.

Next morning we began work in earnest; the land-steward brought his account-books, and various other people came, some to get a dispute settled, some to get arrangements made about other matters. At noon my uncle took me with him to the wing where the two old Baronesses lived, that we might pay our respects to them with all due form. Francis having announced us, we had to wait some time before a little old dame, bent with the weight of her sixty years, and attired in gay-coloured silks, who styled herself the noble ladies' lady-inwaiting, appeared and led us into the sanctuary. There we were received with comical ceremony by the old ladies, whose curious style of dress had gone out of fashion years and years before. I especially was an object of astonishment to them when my uncle, with considerable humour, introduced me as a young lawyer who had come to assist him in his business. Their countenances plainly indicated their belief that, owing to my youth, the welfare of the tenants of R— sitten was placed in jeopardy. Although there was a good deal that was truly ridiculous during the whole of this interview with the old ladies, I was nevertheless still shivering from the terror of the preceding night; I felt as if I had come in contact with an unknown power, or rather as if I had grazed against the outer edge of a circle, one step across which would be enough to plunge me irretrievably into destruction, as though it were only by the exertion of all the power of my will that I should be able to guard myself against that awful dread which never slackens its hold upon you until it ends in incurable insanity. Hence it was that the old Baronesses, with their remarkable towering head-dresses, and their peculiar stuff gowns, tricked off with gay flowers and ribbons, instead of striking me as merely ridiculous, had an appearance that was both ghostly and awe-inspiring. My fancy seemed to glean from their yellow withered faces and blinking eyes, ocular proof of the fact that they had succeeded in establishing themselves on at least a good footing with the ghosts who haunted the castle, as it derived auricular confirmation of the same fact from the wretched French which they croaked, partly between their tightly-closed blue lips and partly through their long thin noses, and also that they themselves possessed the power of setting trouble and dire mischief at work. My uncle, who always had a keen eye for a bit of fun, entangled the old dames in his ironical way in such a mish-mash of nonsensical rubbish that, had I been in any other mood, I should not have known how to swallow down my immoderate laughter; but, as I have just said, the Baronesses and their twaddle were, and continued to be, in my regard, ghostly, so that my old uncle, who was aiming at affording me an especial diversion, glanced across at me time after time utterly astonished. So after dinner, when we were alone together in our room, he burst out, "But in Heaven's name, cousin, tell me what is the matter with you? You don't laugh; you don't talk; you don't eat; and you don't drink. Are you ill, or is anything else the matter with you?" I now hesitated not a moment to tell him circumstantially all my terrible, awful experiences of the previous night I did not conceal anything, and above all I did not conceal that I had drunk a good deal of punch, and had been reading Schiller's "Ghostseer." "This I must confess to," I add, "for only so can I credibly explain how it was that my over-strained and active imagination could create all those ghostly spirits, which only exist within the sphere of my own brain." I fully expected that my uncle would now pepper me well with the stinging pellets of his wit for this my fanciful ghost-seeing; but, on the contrary, he grew very grave, and his eyes became riveted in a set stare upon the floor, until he jerked up his head and said, fixing me with his keen fiery eyes, "Your book I am not acquainted with, cousin; but your ghostly visitants were due neither to it nor to the fumes of the punch. I must tell you that I dreamt exactly the same things that you saw and heard. Like you, I sat in the easy-chair beside the fire (at least I dreamt so); but what was only revealed to you as slight noises I saw and distinctly comprehended with the eye of my mind. Yes, I beheld that foul fiend come in, stealthily and feebly step across to the bricked-up door, and scratch at the wall in hopeless despair until the blood gushed out from beneath his torn finger-nails; then he went downstairs, took a horse out of the stable, and finally put him back again. Did you also hear the cock crowing in a distant farmyard up at the village? You came and awoke me, and I soon resisted the baneful ghost of that terrible man, who is still able to disturb in this fearful way the quiet lives of the living." The old gentleman stopped; and I did not like to ask him further questions, being well aware that he would explain everything to me when he deemed that the proper time was come for doing so. After sitting for a while, deeply absorbed in his own thoughts, he went on, "Cousin, do you think you have courage enough to encounter the ghost again now that you know all that happens,— that is to say, along with me?" Of course I declared that I now felt quite strong enough, and ready for what he wished. "Then let us watch together during the coming night," the old gentleman went on to say. "There is a voice within me telling me that this evil spirit must fly, not so much before the power of my will as before my courage, which rests upon a basis of firm conviction. I feel that it is not at all presumption in me, but rather a good and pious deed, if I venture life and limb to exorcise this foul fiend that is banishing the sons from the old castle of their ancestors. But what am I thinking about? There can be no risk in the case at all, for with such a firm, honest mind and pious trust that I feel I possess, I and everybody cannot fail to be, now and always, victorious over such ghostly antagonists. And yet if, after all, it should be God's will that this evil power be enabled to work me mischief, then you must bear witness, cousin, that I fell in honest Christian fight against the spirit of hell which was here busy about its fiendish work. As for yourself, keep at a distance; no harm will happen to you then."

Our attention was busily engaged with divers kinds of business until evening came. As on the day before, Francis had cleared away the remains of the supper, and brought us our punch. The full moon shone brightly through the gleaming clouds, the sea-waves roared, and the night-wind howled and shook the oriel window till the panes rattled. Although inwardly excited, we forced ourselves to converse on indifferent topics. The old gentleman had placed his striking watch on the table; it struck twelve. Then the door flew open with a terrific bang, and, just as on the preceding night, soft slow footsteps moved stealthily across the hall in a diagonal direction, whilst there were the same sounds of sighing and moaning. My uncle turned pale, but his eyes shone with an unusual brilliance. He rose from his arm-chair, stretching his tall figure up to its full height, so that as he stood there with his left arm propped against his side and with his right stretched out towards the middle of the hall, he had the appearance of a hero issuing his commands. But the sighing and moaning were growing every moment louder and more perceptible, and then the scratching at the wall began more horribly even than on the previous night. My uncle strode forwards straight towards the walled-up door, and his steps were so firm that they echoed along the floor. He stopped immediately in front of the place, where the scratching noise continued to grow worse and worse, and said in a strong solemn voice, such as I had never before heard from his lips, "Daniel, Daniel! what are you doing here at this hour?" Then there was a horrible unearthly scream, followed by a dull thud as if a heavy weight had fallen to the ground. "Seek for pardon and mercy at the throne of the Almighty; that is your place. Away with you from the scenes of this life, in which you can nevermore have part." And as the old gentleman uttered these words in a tone still stronger than before, a feeble wail seemed to pass through the air and die away in the blustering of the storm, which was just beginning to rage. Crossing over to the door, the old gentleman slammed it to, so that the echo rang loudly through the empty anteroom. There was something so supernatural almost in both his language and his gestures that I was deeply struck with awe. On resuming his seat in his arm-chair his face was as if transfigured; he folded his hands and prayed inwardly. In this way several minutes passed, when he asked me in that gentle tone which always went right to my heart, and which he always had so completely at his command, "Well, cousin?" Agitated and shaken by awe, terror, fear, and pious respect and love, I threw myself upon my knees and rained down my warm tears upon the hand he offered me. He clasped me in his arms, and pressing me fervently to his heart said very tenderly, "Now we will go and have a good quiet sleep, good cousin;" and we did so. And as nothing of an unusual nature occurred on the following night, we soon recovered our former cheerfulness, to the prejudice of the old Baronesses;

for though there did still continue to be something ghostly about them and their odd manners, yet it emanated from a diverting ghost which the old gentleman knew how to call up in a droll fashion.

At length, after the lapse of several days, the Baron put in his appearance, along with his wife and a numerous train of servants for the hunting; the guests who had been invited also arrived, and the castle, now suddenly awakened to animation, became the scene of the noisy life and revelry which have been before described. When the Baron came into our hall soon after his arrival, he seemed to be disagreeably surprised at the change in our quarters. Casting an ill-tempered glance towards the bricked-up door, he turned abruptly round and passed his hand across his forehead, as if desirous of banishing some disagreeable recollection. My great-uncle mentioned the damage done to the justice-hall and the adjoining apartments; but the Baron found fault with Francis for not accommodating us with better lodgings, and he good-naturedly requested the old gentleman to order anything he might want to make his new room comfortable; for it was much less satisfactory in this respect than that which he had usually occupied. On the whole, the Baron's bearing towards my old uncle was not merely cordial, but largely coloured by a certain deferential respect, as if the relation in which he stood towards him was that of a younger relative. But this was the sole trait that could in any way reconcile me to his harsh, imperious character, which was now developed more and more every day. As for me, he seemed to notice me but little; if he did notice me at all, he saw in me nothing more than the usual secretary or clerk. On the occasion of the very first important memorandum that I drew up, he began to point out mistakes, as he conceived, in the wording. My blood boiled, and I was about to make a caustic reply, when my uncle interposed, informing him briefly that I did my work exactly in the way he wished, and that in legal matters of this kind he alone was responsible. When we were left alone, I complained bitterly of the Baron, who would, I said, always inspire me with growing aversion. "I assure you, cousin," replied the old gentleman, "that the Baron, notwithstanding his unpleasant manner, is really one of the most excellent and kind-hearted men in the world. As I have already told you, he did not assume these manners until the time he became lord of the entail; previous to then he was a modest, gentle youth. Besides, he is not, after all, so bad as you make him out to be; and further, I should like to know why you are so averse to him." As my uncle said these words he smiled mockingly, and the blood rushed hotly and furiously into my face. I could not pretend to hide from myself — I saw it only too clearly, and felt it too unmistakably — that my peculiar antipathy to the Baron sprang out of the fact that I loved, even to madness, a being who appeared to me to be the loveliest and most fascinating of her sex who had ever trod the earth. This lady was none other than the Baroness herself. Her appearance exercised a powerful and irresistible charm upon me at the very moment of her arrival, when I saw her traversing the apartments in her Russian sable cloak, which fitted close to the exquisite symmetry of her shape, and with a rich veil wrapped about her head. Moreover, the circumstance that the two old aunts, with still more extraordinary gowns and beribboned head-dresses than I had yet seen them wear, were sweeping along one on each side of her and cackling their welcomes in French, whilst the Baroness was looking about her in a way so gentle as to baffle all description, nodding graciously first to one and then to another, and then adding in her flute-like voice a few German words in the pure sonorous dialect of Courland — all this formed a truly remarkable and unusual picture, and my imagination involuntarily connected it with the ghostly midnight visitant,— the Baroness being the angel of light who was to break the ban of the spectral powers of evil. This wondrously lovely lady stood forth in startling reality before my mind's eye. At that time she could hardly be nineteen years of age, and her face, as delicately beautiful as her form, bore the impression of the most angelic good-nature; but what I especially noticed was the indescribable fascination of her dark eyes, for a soft melancholy gleam of aspiration shone in them like dewy moonshine, whilst a perfect elysium of rapture and delight was revealed in her sweet and beautiful smile. She often seemed completely lost in her own thoughts, and at such moments her lovely face was swept by dark and fleeting shadows. Many observers would have concluded that she was affected by some distressing pain; but it rather seemed to me that she was struggling with gloomy apprehensions of a future pregnant with dark misfortunes;

and with these, strangely enough, I connected the apparition of the castle, though I could not give the least explanation of why I did so.

On the morning following the Baron's arrival, when the company assembled to breakfast, my old uncle introduced me to the Baroness; and, as usually happens with people in the frame of mind in which I then was, I behaved with indescribable absurdity. In answer to the beautiful lady's simple inquiries how I liked the castle, &c., I entangled myself in the most extraordinary and nonsensical phrases, so that the old aunts ascribed my embarrassment simply and solely to my profound respect for the noble lady, and thought they were called upon condescendingly to take my part, which they did by praising me in French as a very nice and clever young man, as a garçon très joli (handsome lad). This vexed me; so suddenly recovering my self-possession, I threw out a bonmot in better French than the old dames were mistresses of; whereupon they opened their eyes wide in astonishment, and pampered their long thin noses with a liberal supply of snuff. From the Baroness's turning from me with a more serious air to talk to some other lady, I perceived that my bonmot bordered closely upon folly; this vexed me still more, and I wished the two old ladies to the devil. My old uncle's irony had long before brought me through the stage of the languishing love-sick swain, who in childish infatuation coddles his love-troubles; but I knew very well that the Baroness had made a deeper and more powerful impression upon my heart than any other woman had hitherto done. I saw and heard nothing but her; nevertheless I had a most explicit and unequivocal consciousness that it would be not only absurd, but even utter madness to dream of an amour, albeit I perceived no less clearly the impossibility of gazing and adoring at a distance like a love-lorn boy. Of such conduct I should have been perfectly ashamed. But what I could do, and what I resolved to do, was to become more intimate with this beautiful girl without allowing her to get any glimpse of my real feelings, to drink the sweet poison of her looks and words, and then, when far away from her, to bear her image in my heart for many, many days, perhaps for ever. I was excited by this romantic and chivalric attachment to such a degree, that, as I pondered over it during sleepless nights, I was childish enough to address myself in pathetic monologues, and even to sigh lugubriously, "Seraphina! O Seraphina!" till at last my old uncle woke up and cried, "Cousin, cousin! I believe you are dreaming aloud. Do it by daytime, if you can possibly contrive it, but at night have the goodness to let me sleep." I was very much afraid that the old gentleman, who had not failed to remark my excitement on the Baroness's arrival, had heard the name, and would overwhelm me with his sarcastic wit. But next morning all he said, as we went into the justice-hall, was, "God grant every man the proper amount of common sense, and sufficient watchfulness to keep it well under hand. It's a bad look-out when a man becomes converted into a fantastic coxcomb without so much as a word of warning." Then he took his seat at the great table and added, "Write neatly and distinctly, good cousin, that I may be able to read it without any trouble."

The respect, nay, the almost filial veneration which the Baron entertained towards my uncle, was manifested on all occasions. Thus, at the dinner-table he had to occupy the seat — which many envied him — beside the Baroness; as for me, chance threw me first in one place and then in another; but for the most part, two or three officers from the neighbouring capital were wont to attach me to them, in order that they might empty to their own satisfaction their budget of news and amusing anecdotes, whilst diligently passing the wine about. Thus it happened that for several days in succession I sat at the bottom of the table at a great distance from the Baroness. At length, however, chance brought me nearer to her. Just as the doors of the dining-hall were thrown open for the assembled company, I happened to be in the midst of a conversation with the Baroness's companion and confidante,— a lady no longer in the bloom of youth, but by no means ill-looking, and not without intelligence,— and she seemed to take some interest in my remarks. According to etiquette, it was my duty to offer her my arm, and I was not a little pleased when she took her place quite close to the Baroness, who gave her a friendly nod. It may be readily imagined that all that I now said was intended not only for my fair neighbour, but also mainly for the Baroness. Whether it was that the inward tension of my feelings imparted an especial animation to all I said, at any rate my companion's attention became more riveted with every succeeding moment; in fact, she was at last entirely absorbed in the visions of the kaleidoscopic world which I unfolded to her gaze. As remarked, she was not without intelligence, and it soon came to pass that our conversation, completely independent of the multitude of words spoken by the other guests (which rambled about first to this subject and then to that), maintained its own free course, launching an effective word now and again whither I wanted it. For I did not fail to observe that my companion shot a significant glance or two across to the Baroness, and that the latter took pains to listen to us. And this was particularly the case when the conversation turned upon music and I began to speak with enthusiasm of this glorious and sacred art; nor did I conceal that, despite the fact of my having devoted myself to the dry tedious study of the law, I possessed tolerable skill on the harpsichord, could sing, and had even set several songs to music.

The majority of the company had gone into another room to take coffee and liqueurs; but, unawares, without knowing how it came about, I found myself near the Baroness, who was talking with her confidante. She at once addressed me, repeating in a still more cordial manner and in the tone in which one talks to an acquaintance, her inquiries as to how I liked living in the castle, &c. I assured her that for the first few days, not only the dreary desolation of the situation, but the ancient castle itself had affected me strangely, but even in this mood I had found much of deep interest, and that now my only wish was to be excused from the stirring scenes of the hunt, for I had not been accustomed to them. The Baroness smiled and said, "I can readily believe that this wild life in our fir forests cannot be very congenial to you. You are a musician, and, unless I am utterly mistaken, a poet as well. I am passionately fond of both arts. I can also play the harp a little, but I have to do without it here in R— sitten, for my husband does not like me to bring it with me. Its soft strains would harmonize but ill with the wild shouts of the hunters and the ringing blare of their bugles, which are the only sounds that ought to be heard here. And O heaven! how I should like to hear a little music!" I protested that I would exert all the skill I had at my command to fulfil her wish, for there must surely without doubt be an instrument of some kind in the castle, even though it were only an old harpsichord. Then the Lady Adelheid (the Baroness's confidante) burst out into a silvery laugh and asked, did I not know that within the memory of man no other instrument had ever been heard in the castle except cracked trumpets, and hunting-horns which in the midst of joy would only sound lugubrious notes, and the twanging fiddles, untuned violoncellos, and braying oboes of itinerant musicians. The Baroness reiterated her wish that she should like to have some music, and especially should like to hear me; and both she and Adelheid racked their brains all to no purpose to devise some scheme by which they could get a decent pianoforte brought to the Castle. At this moment old Francis crossed the room. "Here's the man who always can give the best advice, and can procure everything, even things before unheard of and unseen." With these words the Lady Adelheid called him to her, and as she endeavoured to make him comprehend what it was that was wanted, the Baroness listened with her hands clasped and her head bent forward, looking upon the old man's face with a gentle smile. She made a most attractive picture, like some lovely, winsome child that is all eagerness to have a wished-for toy in its hands. Francis, after having adduced in his prolix manner several reasons why it would be downright impossible to procure such a wonderful instrument in such a big hurry, finally stroked his beard with an air of self-flattery and said, "But the land-steward's lady up at the village performs on the manichord, or whatever is the outlandish name they now call it, with uncommon skill, and sings to it so fine and mournful-like that it makes your eyes red, just like onions do, and makes you feel as if you would like to dance with both legs at once." "And you say she has a pianoforte?" interposed Lady Adelheid. "Aye, to be sure," continued the old man; "it comed straight from Dresden; a"—("Oh, that's fine!" interrupted the Baroness)—"a beautiful instrument," went on the old man, "but a little weakly; for not long ago, when the organist began to play on it the hymn 'In all Thy works,'5 he broke it all to pieces, so that"—("Good gracious!" exclaimed both the Baroness and Lady Adelheid)—"so that," went on the old man again, "it had to be taken to R—— to be mended, and cost a lot of money." "But has it come back again?" asked Lady Adelheid impatiently. "Aye, to be sure, my lady, and the steward's lady will reckon it a high honour ——" At this moment the Baron chanced to pass. He looked across at our group rather astonished, and whispered with a sarcastic smile to the Baroness, "So you have to take counsel of Francis again, I see?" The Baroness cast down her eyes blushing, whilst old Francis breaking off terrified, suddenly threw himself into military posture, his head erect, and his arms close and straight down his side. The old aunts came sailing down upon us in their stuff gowns and carried off the Baroness. Lady Adelheid followed her, and I was left alone as if spell-bound. A struggle began to rage within me between my rapturous anticipations of now being able to be near her whom I adored, who completely swayed all my thoughts and feelings, and my sulky ill-humour and annoyance at the Baron, whom I regarded as a barbarous tyrant. If he were not, would the grey-haired old servant have assumed such a slavish attitude?

"Do you hear? Can you see, I say?" cried my great-uncle, tapping me on the shoulder;— we were going upstairs to our own apartments. "Don't force yourself so on the Baroness's attention," he said when we reached the room. "What good can come of it? Leave that to the young fops who like to pay court to ladies; there are plenty of them to do it." I related how it had all come about, and challenged him to say if I had deserved his reproof. His only reply to this, however, was, "Humph! humph!" as he drew on his dressing-gown. Then, having lit his pipe, he took his seat in his easy-chair and began to talk about the adventures of the hunt on the preceding day, bantering me on my bad shots. All was quiet in the castle; all the visitors, both gentlemen and ladies, were

36

busy in their own rooms dressing for the evening. For the musicians with the twanging fiddles, untuned violoncellos, and braying oboes, of whom Lady Adelheid had spoken, were come, and a merrymaking of no less importance than a ball, to be given in the best possible style, was in anticipation. My old uncle, preferring a quiet sleep to such foolish pastimes, stayed in his chamber. I, however, had just finished dressing when there came a light tap at our door, and Francis entered. Smiling in his self-satisfied way, he announced to me that the manichord had just arrived from the land-steward's lady in a sledge, and had been carried into the Baroness's apartments. Lady Adelheid sent her compliments and would I go over at once. It may be conceived how my pulse beat, and also with what a delicious tremor at heart I opened the door of the room in which I was to find her. Lady Adelheid came to meet me with a joyful smile. The Baroness, already in full dress for the ball, was sitting in a meditative attitude beside the mysterious case or box, in which slumbered the music that I was called upon to awaken. When she rose, her beauty shone upon me with such glorious splendour that I stood staring at her unable to utter a word. "Come, Theodore"— (for, according to the kindly custom of the North, which is found again farther south, she addressed everybody by his or her Christian name)—"Come, Theodore," she said pleasantly, "here's the instrument come. Heaven grant it be not altogether unworthy of your skill!" As I opened the lid I was greeted by the rattling of a score of broken strings, and when I attempted to strike a chord, the effect was hideous and abominable, for all the strings which were not broken were completely out of tune. "I doubt not our friend the organist has been putting his delicate little hands upon it again," said Lady Adelheid laughing; but the Baroness was very much annoyed and said, "Oh, it really is a slice of bad luck! I am doomed, I see, never to have any pleasure here." I searched in the case of the instrument, and fortunately found some coils of strings, but no tuning-key anywhere. Hence fresh laments. "Any key will do if the ward will fit on the pegs," I explained; then both Lady Adelheid and the Baroness ran backwards and forwards in gay spirits, and before long a whole magazine of bright keys lay before me on the sounding-board.

Then I set to work diligently, and both the ladies assisted me all they could, trying first one peg and then another. At length one of the tiresome keys fitted, and they exclaimed joyfully, "This will do! it will do!" But when I had drawn the first creaking string up to just proper pitch, it suddenly snapped, and the ladies recoiled in alarm. The Baroness, handling the brittle wires with her delicate little fingers, gave me the numbers as I wanted them, and carefully held the coil whilst I unrolled it. Suddenly one of them coiled itself up again with a whirr, making the Baroness utter an impatient "Oh!" Lady Adelheid enjoyed a hearty laugh, whilst I pursued the tangled coil to the corner of the room. After we had all united our efforts to extract a perfectly straight string from it, and had tried it again, to our mortification it again broke; but at last — at last we found some good coils; the strings began to hold, and gradually the discordant jangling gave place to pure melodious chords. "Ha! it will go! it will go! The instrument is getting in tune!" exclaimed the Baroness, looking at me with her lovely smile. How quickly did this common interest banish all the strangeness and shyness which the artificial manners of social intercourse impose. A kind of confidential familiarity arose between us, which, burning through me like an electric current, consumed the timorous nervousness and constraint which had lain like ice upon my heart. That peculiar mood of diffused melting sadness which is engendered of such love as mine was had quite left me; and accordingly, when the pianoforte was brought into something like tune, instead of interpreting my deeper feelings in dreamy improvisations, as I had intended, I began with those sweet and charming canzonets which have reached us from the South. During this or the other Senza di te (Without thee), or Sentimi idol mio (Hear me, my darling), or Almen se nonpos'io (At least if I cannot), with numberless Morir mi sentos (I feel I am dying), and Addios (Farewell), and O dios! (O Heaven!), a brighter and brighter brilliancy shone in Seraphina's eyes. She had seated herself close beside me at the instrument; I felt her breath fanning my cheek; and as she placed her arm behind me on the chair-back, a white ribbon, getting disengaged from her beautiful ball-dress, fell across my shoulder, where by my singing and Seraphina's soft sighs it was kept in a continual flutter backwards and forwards, like a true love-messenger. It is a wonder how I kept from losing my head.

As I was running my fingers aimlessly over the keys,

thinking of a new song, Lady Adelheid, who had been sitting in one of the corners of the room, ran across to us, and, kneeling down before the Baroness, begged her, as she took both her hands and clasped them to her bosom, "Oh, dear Baroness! darling Seraphina! now you must sing too." To this she replied, "Whatever are you thinking about, Adelheid? How could I dream of letting our virtuoso friend hear such poor singing as mine?" And she looked so lovely, as, like a shy good child, she cast down her eyes and blushed, timidly contending with the desire to sing. That I too added my entreaties can easily be imagined; nor, upon her making mention of some little Courland Volkslieder or popular songs, did I desist from my entreaties until she stretched out her left hand towards the instrument and tried a few notes by way of introduction. I rose to make way for her at the piano, but she would not permit me to do so, asserting that she could not play a single chord, and for that reason, since she would have to sing without accompaniment, her performance would be poor and uncertain. She began in a sweet voice, pure as a bell, that came straight from her heart, and sang a song whose simple melody bore all the characteristics of those Volkslieder which proceed from the lips with such a lustrous brightness, so to speak, that we cannot help perceiving in the glad light which surrounds us our own higher poetic nature. There lies a mysterious charm in the insignificant words of the text which converts them into a hieroglyphic scroll representative of the unutterable emotions which throng our hearts. Who does not know that

Spanish canzonet the substance of which is in words little more than, "With my maiden I embarked on the sea; a storm came on, and my timid maiden was tossed up and down: nay, I will never again embark on the sea with my maiden?" And the Baroness's little song contained nothing more than, "Lately I was dancing with my sweetheart at a wedding; a flower fell out of my hair; he picked it up and gave it me, and said, 'When, sweetheart mine, shall we go to a wedding again?'" When, on her beginning the second verse of the song, I played an arpeggio accompaniment, and further when, in the inspiration which now took possession of me, I at once stole from the Baroness's own lips the melodies of the other songs she sang, I doubtless appeared in her eyes, and in those of the Lady Adelheid, to be one of the greatest of masters in the art of music, for they overwhelmed me with enthusiastic praise. The lights and illuminations from the ball-room, situated in one of the wings of the castle, now shone across into the Baroness's chamber, whilst a discordant bleating of trumpets and French horns announced that it was time to gather for the ball. "Oh, now I must go," said the Baroness. I started up from the pianoforte. "You have afforded me a delightful hour; these have been the pleasantest moments I have ever spent in R— sitten," she added, offering me her hand; and as in the extreme intoxication of delight I pressed it to my lips, I felt her fingers close upon my hand with a sudden convulsive tremor. I do not know how I managed to reach my uncle's chamber, and still less how I got into the ball-room. There was a certain Gascon who was afraid to go into battle since he was all heart, and every wound would be fatal to him. I might be compared to him; and so might everybody else who is in the same mood that I was in; every touch was then fatal. The Baroness's hand — her tremulous fingers — had affected me like a poisoned arrow; my blood was burning in my veins.

On the following morning my old uncle, without asking any direct questions, had soon drawn from me a full account of the hour I had spent in the Baroness's society, and I was not a little abashed when the smile vanished from his lips and the jocular note from his words, and he grew serious all at once, saying, "Cousin, I beg you will resist this folly which is taking such a powerful hold upon you. Let me tell you that your present conduct, as harmless as it now appears, may lead to the most terrible consequences. In your thoughtless fatuity you are standing on a thin crust of ice, which may break under you ere you are aware of it, and let you in with a plunge. I shall take good care not to hold you fast by the coat-tails, for I know you will scramble out again pretty quick, and then, when you are lying sick unto death, you will say, 'I got this little bit of a cold in a dream.' But I warn you that a malignant fever will gnaw at your vitals, and years will pass before you recover yourself, and are a man again. The deuce take your music if you can put it to no better use than to cozen sentimental young women out of their quiet peace of mind." "But," I began, interrupting the old gentleman, "but have I ever thought of insinuating myself as the Baroness's lover?" "You puppy!" cried the old gentleman, "if I thought so

I would pitch you out of this window." At this juncture the Baron entered, and put an end to the painful conversation; and the business to which I now had to turn my attention brought me back from my love-sick reveries, in which I saw and thought of nothing but Seraphina.

In general society the Baroness only occasionally interchanged a few friendly words with me; but hardly an evening passed in which a secret message was not brought to me from Lady Adelheid, summoning me to Seraphina. It soon came to pass that our music alternated with conversations on divers topics. Whenever I and Seraphina began to get too absorbed in sentimental dreams and vague aspirations, the Lady Adelheid, though now hardly young enough to be so naïve and droll as she once was, yet intervened with all sorts of merry and somewhat chaotic nonsense. From several hints she let fall, I soon discovered that the Baroness really had something preying upon her mind, even as I thought I had read in her eyes the very first moment I saw her; and I clearly discerned the hostile influence of the apparition of the castle. Something terrible had happened or was to happen. Although I was often strongly impelled to tell Seraphina in what way I had come in contact with the invisible enemy, and how my old uncle had banished him, undoubtedly for ever, I yet felt my tongue fettered by a hesitation which was inexplicable to myself even, whenever I opened my mouth to speak.

One day the Baroness failed to appear at the dinner table; it was said that she was a little unwell, and could not leave her room. Sympathetic inquiries were addressed to the Baron as to whether her illness was of a grave nature. He smiled in a very disagreeable way, in fact, it was almost like bitter irony, and said, "Nothing more than a slight catarrh, which she has got from our blustering sea-breezes. They can't tolerate any sweet voices; the only sounds they will endure are the hoarse 'Halloos' of the chase." At these words the Baron hurled a keen searching look at me across the table, for I sat obliquely opposite to him. He had not spoken to his neighbour, but to me. Lady Adelheid, who sat beside me, blushed a scarlet red. Fixing her eyes upon the plate in front of her, and scribbling about on it with her fork, she whispered, "And yet you must see Seraphina today; your sweet songs shall today also bring soothing and comfort to her poor heart." Adelheid addressed these words to me; but at this moment it struck me that I was almost apparently entangled in a base and forbidden intrigue with the Baroness, which could only end in some terrible crime. My old uncle's warning fell heavily upon my heart. What should I do? Not see her again? That was impossible so long as I remained in the castle; and even if I might leave the castle and return to K——, I had not the will to do it Oh! I felt only too deeply that I was not strong enough to shake myself out of this dream, which was mocking one with delusive hopes of happiness. Adelheid I almost regarded in the light of a common go-between; I would despise her, and yet, upon second thoughts, I could not help being ashamed of my folly. Had anything ever happened during those blissful evening hours which could in the least degree lead to any nearer relation with Seraphina than was permissible by propriety and morality? How dare I let the thought enter my mind that the Baroness would ever entertain any warm feeling for me? And yet I was convinced of the danger of my situation.

We broke up from dinner earlier than usual, in order to go again after some wolves which had been seen in the fir-wood close by the castle. A little hunting was just the thing I wanted in the excited frame of mind in which I then was. I expressed to my uncle my resolve to accompany the party; he gave me an approving smile and said, "That's right; I am glad you are going out with them for once. I shall stay at home, so you can take my firelock with you, and buckle my whinger round your waist; in case of need it is a good and trusty weapon, if you only keep your presence of mind." That part of the wood in which the wolves were supposed to lie was surrounded by the huntsmen. It was bitterly cold; the wind howled through the firs, and drove the light snow-flakes right in my face, so that when at length it came on to be dusk I could scarcely see six paces before me. Quite benumbed by the cold, I left the place that had been assigned to me and sought shelter deeper in the wood. There, leaning against a tree, with my firelock under my arm, I forgot the wolf-hunt entirely; my thoughts had travelled back to Seraphina's cosy room. After a time shots were heard in the far distance; but at the same moment there was a rustling in the reed-bank, and I saw not ten paces from me a huge wolf about to run past me. I took aim, and fired, but missed. The brute sprang towards me with glaring eyes; I should have been lost had I not had sufficient presence of mind to draw my hunting-knife, and, just as the brute was flying at me, to drive it deep into his throat, so that the blood spurted out over my hand and arm. One of the Baron's keepers, who had stood not far from me, came running up with a loud shout, and at his repeated "Halloo!" all the rest soon gathered round us. The Baron hastened up to me, saying, "For God's sake, you are bleeding — you are bleeding. Are you wounded?" I assured him that I was not Then he turned to the keeper who had stood nearest to me, and overwhelmed him with reproaches for not having shot after me when I missed. And notwithstanding that the man maintained this to have been perfectly impossible, since in the very same moment the wolf had rushed upon me, and any shot would have been at the risk of hitting me, the Baron persisted in saying that he ought to have taken especial care of me as a less experienced hunter. Meanwhile the keepers had lifted up the dead animal; it was one of the largest that had been seen for a long time; and everybody admired my courage and resolution, although to myself what I had done appeared quite natural I had not for a moment thought of the danger I had run. The Baron in particular seemed to take very great interest in the matter; I thought he would never be done asking me whether, though I was not wounded by the brute, I did not fear the ill effects that would follow from the fright As we went back to the castle, the Baron took me by the arm like a friend, and I had to give my firelock to a keeper to carry. He still continued to talk about my heroic deed, so that eventually I came to believe in my own heroism, and lost all my constraint and embarrassment, and felt that I had established myself in the Baron's eyes as a man of courage and uncommon resolution. The schoolboy had passed his examination successfully, was now no longer a schoolboy, and all the submissive nervousness of the schoolboy had left him. I now conceived I had earned a right to try and gain Seraphina's favour. Everybody knows of course what ridiculous combinations the fancy of a love-sick youth is capable of. In the castle, over the smoking punchbowl, by the fireside, I was the hero of the hour. Besides myself the Baron was the only one of the party who had killed a wolf — also a formidable one; the rest had to be content with ascribing their bad shots to the weather and the darkness, and with relating thrilling stories of their former exploits in hunting and the dangers they had escaped. I thought, too, that I might reap an especial share of praise and admiration from my old uncle as well; and so, with a view to this end, I related to him my adventure at pretty considerable length, nor did I forget to paint the savage brute's wild and bloodthirsty appearance in very startling colours. The old gentleman, however, only laughed in my face and said, "God is powerful even in the weak."

Tired of drinking and of the company, I was going quietly along the corridor towards the justice-hall when I saw a figure with a light slip in before me. On entering the hall I saw it was Lady Adelheid. "This is the way we have to wander about like ghosts or night-walkers in order to catch you, my brave slayer of wolves," she whispered, taking my arm. The words "ghosts" and "sleep-walkers," pronounced in the place where we were, fell like lead upon my heart; they immediately brought to my recollection the ghostly apparitions of those two awful nights. As then, so now, the wind came howling in from the sea in deep organ-like cadences, rattling the oriel windows again and again and whistling fearfully through them, whilst the moon cast her pale gleams exactly upon the mysterious part of the wall where the scratching had been heard. I fancied I discerned stains of blood upon it. Doubtless Lady Adelheid, who still had hold of my hand, must have felt the cold icy shiver which ran through me. "What's the matter with you?" she whispered softly; "what's the matter with you? You are as cold as marble. Come, I will call you back into life. Do you know how very impatient the Baroness is to see you? And until she does see you she will not believe that the ugly wolf has not really bitten you. She is in a terrible state of anxiety about you. Why, my friend,— oh! how have you awakened this interest in the little Seraphina? I have never seen her like this. Ah!— so now the pulse is beginning to prickle; see how quickly the dead man comes to life! Well, come along — but softly, still! Come, we must go to the little Baroness." I suffered myself to be led away in silence. The way in which Adelheid spoke of the Baroness seemed to me undignified, and the innuendo of an understanding between us positively shameful. When I entered the room along with Adelheid, Seraphina, with a low-breathed "Oh!" advanced three or four paces quickly to meet me; but then, as if recollecting herself, she stood still in the middle of the room. I ventured to take her hand and press it to my lips. Allowing it to rest in mine, she asked, "But, for Heaven's sake! is it your business to meddle with wolves? Don't you know that the fabulous days of Orpheus and Amphion are long past, and that wild beasts have quite lost all respect for even the most admirable of singers?" But this gleeful turn, by which the Baroness at once effectually guarded against all misinterpretation of her warm interest in me, I was put immediately into the proper key and the proper mood. Why I did not take my usual place at the pianoforte I cannot explain, even to myself, nor why I sat down beside the Baroness on the sofa. Her question, "And what were you doing then to get into danger?" was an indication of our tacit agreement that conversation, not music, was to engage our attention for that evening. After I had narrated my adventure in the wood, and mentioned the warm interest which the Baron had taken in it, delicately hinting that I had not thought him capable of so much feeling, the Baroness began in a tender and almost melancholy tone, "Oh! how violent and rude you must think the Baron; but I assure you it is only whilst we are living within these gloomy, ghostly walls, and during the time there is hunting going on in the dismal fir-forests, that his character completely changes, at least his outward behaviour does. What principally disquiets him in this unpleasant way is the thought, which constantly haunts him, that something terrible will happen here. And that undoubtedly accounts for the fact of his being so greatly agitated by your adventure, which fortunately has had no ill consequences. He won't have the meanest of his servants exposed to danger, if he knows it, still less a new-won friend whom he has come to like; and I am perfectly certain that Gottlieb, whom he blames for having left you in the lurch, will be punished; even if he escapes being locked up in a dungeon, he will yet have to suffer the punishment, so mortifying to a hunter, of going out the next time there is a hunt with only a club in his hand instead of a rifle. The circumstance that hunts like those which are held here are always attended with danger, and the fact that the Baron, though always fearing some sad accident, is yet so fond of hunting that he cannot desist from provoking the demon of mischief, make his existence here a kind of conflict, the ill effects of which I also have to feel. Many queer stories are current about his ancestor who established the entail; and I know myself that there is some dark family secret locked within these walls like a horrible ghost which drives away the owners, and makes it impossible for them to bear with it longer than a few weeks at a time — and that only amid a tumult of jovial guests. But I— Oh! how lonely I am in the midst of this noisy, merry company! And how the ghostly influences which breathe upon me from the walls stir and excite my very heart! You, my dear friend, have given me, through your musical skill, the first cheerful moments I have spent here. How can I thank you sufficiently for your kindness!" I kissed the hand she offered to me, saying, that even on the very first day, or rather during the very first night, I had experienced the ghostliness of the place in all its horrors. The Baroness fixed her staring eyes upon my face, as I went on to describe the ghostly character of the building, discernible everywhere throughout the castle, particularly in the decorations of the justice-hall, and to speak of the roaring of the wind from the sea, &c. Possibly my voice and my expressions indicated that I had something more in my mind than what I said; at any rate when I concluded, the Baroness cried vehemently, "No, no; something dreadful has happened to you in that hall, which I never enter without shuddering. I beg you — pray, pray, tell me all."

Seraphina's face had grown deadly pale; and I saw plainly that it would be more advisable to give her a faithful account of all that I had experienced than to leave her excited imagination to conjure up some apparition that might perhaps, in a way I could not foresee, be far more horrible than what I had actually encountered. As she listened to me her fear and strained anxiety increased from moment to moment; and when I mentioned the scratching on the wall she screamed, "It's horrible! Yes, yes, it's in that wall that the awful secret is concealed!" But as I went on to describe with what spiritual power and superiority of will my old uncle had banished the ghost, she sighed deeply, as though she had shaken off a heavy burden that had weighed oppressively upon her. She leaned back in the sofa and held her hands before her face. Now I first noticed that Adelheid had left us. A considerable pause ensued, and as Seraphina still continued silent, I softly rose, and going to the pianoforte, endeavoured in swelling chords to invoke the bright spirits of consolation to come and deliver Seraphina from the dark influence to which my narration had subjected her. Then I soon began to sing as softly as I was able one of the Abbé Steffani's6 canzonas. The melancholy strains of the Ochi, perchè piangete (O eyes, why weep you?) roused Seraphina out of her reverie, and she listened to me with a gentle smile upon her face, and bright pearl-like tears in her eyes. How am I to account for it that I kneeled down before her, that she bent over towards me, that I threw my arms about her, that a long ardent kiss was imprinted on my lips? How am I to account for it that I did not lose my senses when she drew me softly towards her, how that I tore myself from her arms, and, quickly rising to my feet, hurried to the pianoforte? Turning from me, the Baroness took a few steps towards the window, then she turned round again and approached me with an air of almost proud dignity, which was not at all usual with her. Looking me straight in the face, she said, "Your uncle is the most worthy old man I know; he is the guardian-angel of our family. May he include me in his pious prayers!" I was unable to utter a word; the subtle poison that I had imbibed with her kiss burned and boiled in every pulse and nerve. Lady Adelheid came in. The violence of my inward conflict burst out at length in a passionate flood of tears, which I was unable to repress. Adelheid looked at me with wonder and smiled dubiously;— I could have murdered her. The Baroness gave me her hand, and said with inexpressible gentleness, "Farewell, my dear friend. Fare you right well; and remember that nobody perhaps has ever understood your music better than I have. Oh! these notes! they will echo long, long in my heart." I forced myself to utter a few stupid, disconnected words, and hurried up to my uncle's room. The old gentleman had already gone to bed. I stayed in the hall, and falling upon my knees, I wept aloud; I called upon my beloved by name, I gave myself up completely and regardlessly to all the absurd folly of a love-sick lunatic, until at last the extravagant noise I made awoke my uncle. But his loud call, "Cousin, I believe you have gone cranky, or else you're having another tussle with a wolf. Be off to bed with you if you will be so very kind"— these words compelled me to enter his room, where I got into bed with the fixed resolve to dream only of Seraphina.

It would be somewhere past midnight when I thought I heard distant voices, a running backwards and forwards, and an opening and banging of doors — for I had not yet fallen asleep. I listened attentively; I heard footsteps approaching the corridor; the hall door was opened, and soon there came a knock at our door. "Who is there?" I cried. A voice from without answered, "Herr Justitiarius, Herr Justitiarius, wake up, wake up!" I recognised Francis's voice, and as I asked, "Is the castle on fire?" the old gentleman woke up in his turn and asked, "Where — where is there a fire? Is it that cursed apparition again? where is it?" "Oh! please get up, Herr Justitiarius," said Francis, "Please get up; the Baron wants you." "What does the Baron want me for?" inquired my uncle further; "what does he want me for at this time of night? does he not know that all law business goes to bed along with the lawyer, and sleeps as soundly as he does?" "Oh!" cried Francis, now anxiously; "please, Herr Justitiarius, good sir, please get up. My lady the Baroness is dying." I started up with a cry of dismay. "Open the door for Francis," said the old gentleman to me. I stumbled about the room almost distracted, and could find neither door nor lock; my uncle had to come and help me. Francis came in, his face pale and troubled, and lit the candles. We had scarcely thrown on our clothes when we heard the Baron calling in the hall, "Can I speak to you, good V——?" "But what have you dressed for, cousin? the Baron only wanted me," asked the old gentleman, on the point of going out. "I must go down — I must see her and then die," I replied tragically, and as if my heart were rent by hopeless grief. "Ay, just so; you are right, cousin," he said, banging the door to in my face, so that the hinges creaked, and locking it on the outside. At the first moment, deeply incensed at this restraint, I thought of bursting the door open; but quickly reflecting that this would entail the disagreeable consequences of a piece of outrageous insanity, I resolved to await the old gentleman's return; then however, let the cost be what it might, I would escape his watchfulness. I heard him talking vehemently with the Baron, and several times distinguished my own name, but could not make out anything further. Every moment my position grew more intolerable. At length I heard that some one brought a message to the Baron, who immediately hurried off. My old uncle entered the room again. "She is dead!" I cried, running towards him, "And you are a stupid fool," he interrupted coolly; then he laid hold upon me and forced me into a chair. "I must go down," I cried, "I must go down and see her, even though it cost me my life." "Do so, good cousin," said he, locking the door, taking out the key, and putting it in his pocket. I now flew into a perfectly frantic rage; stretching out my hand towards the rifle, I screamed, "If you don't instantly open the door I will send this bullet through my brains." Then the old gentleman planted himself immediately in front of me, and fixing his keen piercing eyes upon me said, "Boy, do you think you can frighten me with your idle threats? Do you think I should set much value on your life if you can go and throw it away in childish folly like a broken plaything? What have you to do with the Baron's wife? who has given you the right to insinuate yourself, like a tiresome puppy, where you have no claim to be, and where you are not wanted? do you wish to go and act the love-sick swain at the solemn hour of death?" I sank back in my chair utterly confounded After a while the old gentleman went on more gently, "And now let me tell you that this pretended illness of the Baroness is in all probability nothing. Lady Adelheid always loses her head at the least little thing. If a rain-drop falls upon her nose, she screams, 'What fearful weather it is!' Unfortunately the noise penetrated to the old aunts, and they, in the midst of unseasonable floods of tears, put in an appearance armed with an entire arsenal of strengthening drops, elixirs of life, and the deuce knows what. A sharp fainting-fit"—— The old gentleman checked himself; doubtless he observed the struggle that was going on within me. He took a few turns through the room; then again planting himself in front of me, he had a good hearty laugh and said, "Cousin, cousin, what nonsensical folly have you now got in your head? Ah well! I suppose it can't be helped; the devil is to play his pretty games here in divers sorts of ways. You have tumbled very nicely into his clutches, and now he's making you dance to a sweet tune," He again took a few turns up and down, and again went on, "It's no use to think of sleep now; and it occurred to me that we might have a pipe, and so spend the few hours that are left of the darkness and the night." With these words he took a clay pipe from the cupboard, and proceeded to fill it slowly and carefully, humming a song to himself; then he rummaged about amongst a heap of papers, until he found a sheet, which he picked out and rolled into a spill and lighted. Blowing the tobacco-smoke from him in thick clouds, he said, speaking between his teeth, "Well, cousin, what was that story about the wolf?"

I know not how it was, but this calm, quiet behaviour of the old gentleman operated strangely upon me. I seemed to be no longer in R— sitten, and the Baroness was so far, far distant from me that I could only reach her on the wings of thought. The old gentleman's last question, however, annoyed me. "But do you find my hunting exploit so amusing?" I broke in,—"so well fitted for banter?" "By no means," he rejoined, "by no means, cousin mine; but you've no idea what a comical face such a whipper-snapper as you cuts, and how ludicrously he acts as well, when Providence for once in a while honours him by putting him in the way to meet with something out of the usual run of things. I once had a college friend who was a quiet, sober fellow, and always on good terms with himself. By accident he became entangled in an affair of honour,— I say by accident, because he himself was never in any way aggressive; and although most of the fellows looked upon him as a poor thing, as a poltroon, he yet showed so much firm and resolute courage in this affair as greatly to excite everybody's admiration. But from that time onwards he was also completely changed. The sober and industrious youth became a bragging, insufferable bully. He was always drinking and rioting, and fighting about all sorts of childish trifles, until he was run through in a duel by the Senior7 of an exclusive corps. I merely tell you the story, cousin; you are at liberty to think what you please about it But to return to the Baroness and her illness"—— At this moment light footsteps were heard in the hall; I fancied, too, there was an unearthly moaning in the air. "She is dead!" the thought shot through me like a fatal flash of lightning. The old gentleman quickly rose to his feet and called out, "Francis, Francis!" "Yes, my good Herr Justitiarius," he replied from without. "Francis," went on my uncle, "rake the fire together a bit in the grate, and if you can manage it, you had better make us a good cup or two of tea." "It is devilish cold," and he turned to me, "and I think we had better go and sit round the fire and talk a little." He opened the door, and I followed him mechanically. "How are things going on below?" he asked. "Oh!" replied Francis; "there was not much the matter. The Lady Baroness is all right again, and ascribes her bit of a fainting-fit to a bad dream." I was going to break out into an extravagant manifestation of joy and gladness, but a stern glance from my uncle kept me quiet "And yet, after all, I think it would be better if we lay down for an hour or two. You need not mind about the tea, Francis." "As you think well, Herr Justitiarius," replied Francis, and he left the room with the wish that we might have a good night's rest, albeit the cocks were already crowing. "See here, cousin," said the old gentleman, knocking the ashes out of his pipe on the grate, "I think, cousin, that it's a very good thing no harm has happened to you either from wolves or from loaded rifles." I now saw things in the right light, and was ashamed at myself to have thus given the old gentleman good grounds for treating me like a spoiled child.

Next morning he said to me, "Be so good as to step down, good cousin, and inquire how the Baroness is. You need only ask for Lady Adelheid; she will supply you with a full budget, I have no doubt" You may imagine how eagerly I hastened downstairs. But just as I was about to give a gentle knock at the door of the Baroness's anteroom, the Baron came hurriedly out of the same. He stood still in astonishment, and scrutinised me with a gloomy searching look. "What do you want here?" burst from his lips. Notwithstanding that my heart beat, I controlled myself and replied in a firm tone, "To inquire on my uncle's behalf how my lady, the Baroness, is?" "Oh! it was nothing — one of her usual nervous attacks. She is now having a quiet sleep, and will, I am sure, make her appearance at the dinner-table quite well and cheerful.

Tell him that — tell him that." This the Baron said with a certain degree of passionate vehemence, which seemed to me to imply that he was more concerned about the Baroness than he was willing to show. I turned to go back to my uncle, when the Baron suddenly seized my arm and said, whilst his eyes flashed fire, "I have a word or two to say to you, young man." Here I saw the deeply injured husband before me, and feared there would be a scene which would perhaps end ignominiously for me. I was unarmed; but at that moment I remembered I had in my pocket the ingeniously-made hunting-knife which my uncle had presented to me after we got to R— sitten. I now followed the Baron, who led the way rapidly, with the determination not even to spare his life if I ran any risk of being treated dishonourably.

We entered the Baron's own room, the door of which he locked behind him. Now he began to pace restlessly backwards and forwards, with his arms folded one over the other; then he stopped in front of me and repeated, "I have a word or two to say to you, young man." I had wound myself up to a pitch of most daring courage, and I replied, raising my voice, "I hope they will be words which I may hear without resentment." He stared hard at me in astonishment, as though he had failed to understand me. Then, fixing his eyes gloomily upon the floor, he threw his arms behind his back, and again began to stride up and down the room. He took down a rifle and put the ramrod down the barrel to see whether it were loaded or not. My blood boiled in my veins; grasping my knife, I stepped close up to him, so as to make it impossible for him to take aim at me. "That's a handsome weapon," he said, replacing the rifle in the corner. I retired a few paces, the Baron following me. Slapping me on the shoulder, perhaps a little more violently than was necessary, he said, "I daresay I seem to you, Theodore, to be excited and irritable; and I really am so, owing to the anxieties of a sleepless night. My wife's nervous attack was not in the least dangerous; that I now see plainly. But here — here in this castle, which is haunted by an evil spirit, I always dread something terrible happening; and then it's the first time she has been ill here. And you — you alone were to blame for it." "How that can possibly be I have not the slightest conception," I replied calmly. "I wish," continued the Baron, "I wish that damned piece of mischief, my steward's wife's instrument, were chopped up into a thousand pieces, and that you — but no, no; it was to be so, it was inevitably to be so, and I alone am to blame for all. I ought to have told you, the moment you began to play music in my wife's room, of the whole state of the case, and to have informed you of my wife's temper of mind." I was about to speak; "Let me go on," said the Baron, "I must prevent your forming any rash judgment. You probably regard me as an uncultivated fellow, averse to the arts; but I am not so by any means. There is a particular consideration, however, based upon deep conviction, which constrains me to forbid the introduction here as far as possible of such music as can powerfully affect any person's mind, and to this I of course am no exception. Know that my wife suffers from a morbid excitability, which will finally destroy all the happiness of her life. Within these strange walls she is never quit of that strained over-excited condition, which at other times occurs but temporarily, and then generally as the forerunner of a serious illness. You will ask me, and quite reasonably too, why I do not spare my delicate wife the necessity of coming to live in this weird castle, and mix amongst the wild confusion of a hunting-party. Well, call it weakness — be it so; in a word, I cannot bring myself to leave her behind. I should be tortured by a thousand fears, and quite incapable of any serious business, for I am perfectly sure that I should be haunted everywhere, in the justice-hall as well as in the forest, by the most horrid ideas of all kinds of fatal mischief happening to her. And, on the other hand, I believe that the sort of life led here cannot fail to operate upon the weakly woman like strengthening chalybeate waters. By my soul, the sea-breezes, sweeping keenly after their peculiar fashion through the fir-trees, and the deep baying of the hounds, and the merry ringing notes of our hunting-horns must get the better of all your sickly languishing sentimentalisings at the piano, which no man ought play in that way. I tell you, you are deliberately torturing my wife to death." These words he uttered with great emphasis, whilst his eyes flashed with a restless fire. The blood mounted to my head; I made a violent gesture against the Baron with my hand; I was about to speak, but he cut me short "I know what you are going to say," he began, "I know what you are going to say, and I repeat that you are going the right road to kill my wife. But that you intended this I cannot of course for a moment maintain; and yet you will understand that I must put a stop to the thing. In short, by your playing and singing you work her up to a high pitch of excitement, and then, when she drifts without anchor and rudder on the boundless sea of dreams and visions and vague aspirations which your music, like some vile charm, has summoned into existence, you plunge her down into the depths of horror with a tale about a fearful apparition which you say came and played pranks with you up in the justice-hall. Your great-uncle has told me everything; but, pray, repeat to me all you saw, or did not see, heard, felt, divined by instinct."

I braced myself up and narrated calmly how everything had happened from beginning to end, the Baron merely interposing at intervals a few words expressive of his astonishment. When I came to the part where my old uncle had met the ghost with trustful courage and had exorcised him with a few powerful words, the Baron clasped his hands, raised them folded towards Heaven, and said with deep emotion, "Yes, he is the guardian-angel of the family. His mortal remains shall rest in the vault of my ancestors." When I finished my narration, the Baron murmured to himself, "Daniel, Daniel, what are you doing here at this hour?" as he folded his arms and strode up and down the room. "And was that all, Herr Baron?" I asked, making a movement as though I would retire. Starting up as if out of a dream, the Baron took me kindly by the hand and said, "Yes, my good friend, my wife, whom you have dealt so hardly by without intending it — you must cure her again; you alone can do

62

so." I felt I was blushing, and had I stood opposite a mirror should undoubtedly have seen in it a very blank and absurd face. The Baron seemed to exult in my embarrassment; he kept his eyes fixed intently upon my face, smiling with perfectly galling irony. "How in the world can I cure her?" I managed to stammer out at length with an effort "Well," he said, interrupting me, "you have no dangerous patient to deal with at any rate. I now make an express claim upon your skill. Since the Baroness has been drawn into the enchanted circle of your music, it would be both foolish and cruel to drag her out of it all of a sudden. Go on with your music therefore. You will always be welcome during the evening hours in my wife's apartments. But gradually select a more energetic kind of music, and effect a clever alternation of the cheerful sort with the serious; and above all things, repeat your story of the fearful ghost very very often. The Baroness will grow familiar with it; she will forget that a ghost haunts this castle; and the story will have no stronger effect upon her than any other tale of enchantment which is put before her in a romance or a ghost-story book. Pray, do this, my good friend." With these words the Baron left me. I went away. I felt as if I were annihilated, to be thus humiliated to the level of a foolish and insignificant child. Fool that I was to suppose that jealousy was stirring his heart! He himself sends me to Seraphina; he sees in me only the blind instrument which, after he has made use of it, he can throw away if he thinks well. A few minutes previously I had really feared the Baron; deep down within my heart lurked the consciousness of guilt; but it was a consciousness which allowed me to feel distinctly the beauty of the higher life for which I was ripe. Now all had disappeared in the blackness of night; and I saw only the stupid boy who in childish obstinacy had persisted in taking the paper crown which he had put on his hot temples for a real golden one. I hurried away to my uncle, who was waiting for me. "Well, cousin, why have you been so long? Where have you been staying?" he cried as soon as he saw me. "I have been having some words with the Baron!" I quickly replied, carelessly and in a low voice, without being able to look at the old gentleman. "God damn it all," said he, feigning astonishment "Good gracious, boy! that's just what I thought. I suppose the Baron has challenged you, cousin?" The ringing peal of laughter which the old gentleman immediately afterwards broke out into taught me that this time too, as always, he had seen me through and through. I bit my lip, and durst not speak a word, for I knew very well that it would only be the signal for the old gentleman to overwhelm me beneath the torrent of teasing which was already hovering on the tip of his tongue.

The Baroness appeared at the dinner-table in an elegant morning-robe, the dazzling whiteness of which exceeded that of fresh-fallen snow. She looked worn and low-spirited; but she began to speak in her soft and melodious accents, and on raising her dark eyes there shone a sweet and yearning look full of aspiration in their voluptuous glow, and a fugitive blush flitted across her lily-white cheeks. She was more beautiful than ever. But who can fathom the follies of a young man who has got too hot blood in his head and heart? The bitter pique which the Baron had stirred up within me I transferred to the Baroness. The entire business seemed to me like a foul mystification; and I would now show that I was possessed of alarmingly good common-sense and also of extraordinary sagacity. Like a petulant child, I shunned the Baroness and escaped Adelheid when she pursued me, and found a place where I wished, right at the bottom end of the table between the two officers, with whom I began to carouse right merrily. We kept our glasses going gaily during dessert, and I was, as so frequently is the case in moods like mine, extremely noisy and loud in my joviality. A servant brought me a plate with some bonbons on it, with the words, "From Lady Adelheid." I took them; and observed on one of them, scribbled in pencil, "and Seraphina." My blood coursed tumultuously in my veins. I sent a glance in Adelheid's direction, which she met with a most sly and archly cunning look; and taking her glass in her hand, she gave me a slight nod. Almost mechanically I murmured to myself, "Seraphina!" then taking up my glass in my turn, I drained it at a single draught. My glance fell across in her direction; I perceived that she also had drunk at the very same moment and was setting down her glass. Our eyes met, and a malignant demon whispered in my ear, "Unhappy wretch, she does love you!" One of the guests now rose, and, in conformity with the custom of the North, proposed the health of the lady of the house. Our glasses rang in the midst of a tumult of joy. My heart was torn with rapture and despair; the wine burned like fire within me; everything spun round in circles; I felt as if I must hasten and throw myself at her feet and there sigh out my life. "What's the matter with you, my friend?" asked my neighbour, thus recalling me to myself; but Seraphina had left the hall. We rose from the table. I was making for the door, but Adelheid held me fast, and began to talk about divers matters; I neither heard nor understood a single word. She grasped both my hands and, laughing, shouted something in my ear. I remained dumb and motionless, as though affected by catalepsy. All I remember is that I finally took a glass of liqueur out of Adelheid's hand in a mechanical way and drank it off, and then I recollect being alone in a window, and after that I rushed out of the hall, down the stairs, and ran out into the wood. The snow was falling in thick flakes; the fir-trees were moaning as they waved to and fro in the wind. Like a maniac I ran round and round in wide circles, laughing and screaming loudly, "Look, look and see. Aha! Aha! The devil is having a fine dance with the boy who thought he would taste of strictly forbidden fruit!" Who can tell what would have been the end of my mad prank if I had not heard my name called loudly from the outside of the wood? The storm had abated; the moon shone out brightly through the broken clouds; I heard dogs barking, and perceived a dark figure approaching me. It was the old man Francis. "Why, why, my good Herr Theodore," he began, "you have quite lost your way in the rough snow-storm. The Herr Justitiarius is awaiting you with much impatience." I followed the old man in silence. I found my great-uncle working in the justice-hall. "You have done well," he cried, on seeing me, "you have done a very wise thing to go out in the open air a little and get cool. But don't drink quite so much wine; you are far too young, and it's not good for you." I did not utter a word in reply, and also took my place at the table in silence. "But now tell me, good cousin, what it was the Baron really wanted you for?" I told him all, and concluded by stating that I would not lend myself for the doubtful cure which the Baron had proposed. "And it would not be practicable," the old gentleman interrupted, "for tomorrow morning early we set off home, cousin." And so it was that I never saw Seraphina again.

As soon as we arrived in K—— my old uncle complained that he felt the effects of the wearying journey this time more than ever. His moody silence, broken only by violent outbreaks of the worst possible ill-humour, announced the return of his attacks of gout. One day I was suddenly called in; I found the old gentleman confined to his bed and unable to speak, suffering from a paralytic stroke. He held a letter in his hand, which he had crumpled up tightly in a spasmodic fit. I recognised the hand-writing of the land-steward of R—— sitten; but, quite upset by my trouble, I did not venture to take the letter out of the old gentleman's hand. I did not doubt that his end was near. But his pulse began to beat again, even before the physician arrived; the old gentleman's remarkably tough constitution resisted the mortal attack, although he was in his seventieth year. That selfsame day the doctor pronounced him out of danger.

We had a more severe winter than usual; this was followed

by a rough and stormy spring; and hence it was more the gout — a consequence of the inclemency of the season — than his previous accident which kept him for a long time confined to his bed. During this period he made up his mind to retire altogether from all kinds of business. He transferred his office of Justitiarius to others; and so I was cut off from all hope of ever again going to R— sitten. The old gentleman would allow no one to attend him but me; and it was to me alone that he looked for all amusement and every cheerful diversion. And though, in the hours when he was free from pain, his good spirits returned, and he had no lack of broad jests, even making mention of hunting exploits, so that I fully expected every minute to hear him make a butt of my heroic deed, when I had killed the wolf with my whinger, yet never once did he allude to our visit to R— sitten, and as may well be imagined, I was very careful, from natural shyness, not to lead him directly up to the subject. My harassing anxiety and continual attendance upon the old gentleman had thrust Seraphina's image into the background. But as soon as his sickness abated somewhat, my thoughts returned with more liveliness to that moment in the Baroness's room, which I now looked upon as a star — a bright star — that had set, for me at least, for ever. An occurrence which now happened, by making me shudder with an ice-cold thrill as at sight of a visitant from the world of spirits, revived all the pain I had formerly felt. One evening, as I was opening the pocket-book which I had carried whilst at R— sitten, there fell out of the papers I was unfolding a dark curl, wrapped about with a white ribbon; I immediately recognised it as Seraphina's hair. But, on examining the ribbon more closely, I distinctly perceived the mark of a spot of blood on it! Perhaps Adelheid had skilfully contrived to secrete it about me during the moments of conscious insanity by which I had been affected during the last days of our visit; but why was the spot of blood there? It excited forebodings of something terrible in my mind, and almost converted this too pastoral love-token into an awful admonition, pointing to a passion which might entail the expenditure of precious blood. It was the same white ribbon that had fluttered about me in light wanton sportiveness as it were the first time I sat near Seraphina, and which Mysterious Night had stamped as an emblem of mortal injury. Boys ought not to play with weapons with the dangerous properties of which they are not familiar.

At last the storms of spring had ceased to bluster, and summer asserted her rights; and if the cold had formerly been unbearable, so now too was the heat when July came in. The old gentleman visibly gathered strength, and following his usual custom, went out to a garden in the suburbs. One still, warm evening, as we sat in the sweet-smelling jasmine arbour, he was in unusually good spirits, and not, as was generally the case, overflowing with sarcasm and irony, but in a gentle and almost soft and melting mood. "Cousin," he began, "I don't know how it is, but I feel so nice and warm and comfortable all over today; I have not felt like it for many years. I believe it is an augury that I shall die soon."

I exerted myself to drive these gloomy thoughts from his mind. "Never mind, cousin," he said, "in any case I'm not long for this world; and so I will now discharge a debt I owe you. Do you still remember our autumn in R— sitten?" This question thrilled through me like a lightning-flash, so before I was able to make any reply he continued, "It was Heaven's will that your entrance into that castle should be signalised by memorable circumstances, and that you should become involved against your own will in the deepest secrets of the house. The time has now come when you must learn all. We have often enough talked about things which you, cousin, rather dimly guessed at than really understood. In the alternation of the seasons nature represents symbolically the cycle of human life. That is a trite remark; but I interpret it differently from everybody else. The dews of spring fall, summer's vapours fade away, and it is the pure atmosphere of autumn which clearly reveals the distant landscape, and then finally earthly existence is swallowed in the night of winter. I mean that the government of the Power Inscrutable is more plainly revealed in the clear-sightedness of old age. It is granted glimpses of the promised land, the pilgrimage to which begins with the death on earth. How clearly do I see at this moment the dark destiny of that house, to which I am knit by firmer ties than blood relationship can weave! Everything lies disclosed to the eyes of my spirit. And yet the things which I now see, in the form in which I see them — the essential substance of them, that is — this I cannot tell you in words; for no man's tongue is able to do so. But listen, my son, I will tell you as well as I am able, and do you think it is some remarkable story that might really happen; and lay up carefully in your soul the knowledge that the mysterious relations into which you ventured to enter, not perhaps without being summoned, might have ended in your destruction — but — that's all over now."

The history of the R—— entail, which my old uncle told me, I retain so faithfully in my memory even now that I can almost repeat it in his own words (he spoke of himself in the third person).

One stormy night in the autumn of 1760 the servants of R— sitten were startled out of the midst of their sleep by a terrific crash, as if the whole of the spacious castle had tumbled into a thousand pieces. In a moment everybody was on his legs; lights were lit; the house-steward, his face deadly pale with fright and terror, came up panting with his keys; but as they proceeded through the passages and halls and rooms, suite after suite, and found all safe, and heard in the appalling silence nothing except the creaking rattle of the locks, which occasioned some difficulty in opening, and the ghost-like echo of their own footsteps, they began one and all to be utterly astounded. Nowhere was there the least trace of damage. The old house-steward was impressed by an ominous feeling of apprehension. He went up into the great Knight's Hall, which had a small cabinet adjoining where Freiherr Roderick von R—— used to sleep when engaged in making his astronomical observations. Between the door of this cabinet and that of a second was a postern, leading through a narrow passage immediately into the astronomical tower. But directly Daniel (that was the house-steward's name) opened this postern, the storm, blustering and howling terrifically, drove a heap of rubbish and broken pieces of stones all over him, which made him recoil in terror; and, dropping the candles, which went out with a hiss on the floor, he screamed, "O God! O God! The Baron! he's miserably dashed to pieces!" At the same moment he heard sounds of lamentation proceeding from the Freiherr's sleeping-cabinet, and on entering it he saw the servants gathered around their master's corpse. They had found him fully dressed and more magnificently than on any previous occasion, and with a calm earnest look upon his unchanged countenance, sitting in his large and richly decorated arm-chair as though resting after severe study. But his rest was the rest of death. When day dawned it was seen that the crowning turret of the tower had fallen in. The huge square stones had broken through the ceiling and floor of the observatory-room, and then, carrying down in front of them a powerful beam that ran across the tower, they had dashed in with redoubled impetus the lower vaulted roof, and dragged down a portion of the castle walls and of the narrow connecting-passage. Not a single step could be taken beyond the postern threshold without risk of falling at least eighty feet into a deep chasm.

The old Freiherr had foreseen the very hour of his death, and had sent intelligence of it to his sons. Hence it happened that the very next day saw the arrival of Wolfgang, Freiherr von R——, eldest son of the deceased, and now lord of the entail. Relying confidently upon the probable truth of the old man's foreboding, he had left Vienna, which city he chanced to have reached in his travels, immediately he received the ominous letter, and hastened to R— sitten as fast as he could travel. The house-steward had draped the great hall in black, and had had the old Freiherr laid out in the clothes in which he had been found, on a magnificent state-bed, and this he had surrounded with tall silver candlesticks with burning wax-candles. Wolfgang ascended the stairs, entered the hall, and approached close to his father's corpse, without speaking a word. There he stood with his arms folded on his chest, gazing with a fixed and gloomy look and with knitted brows, into his father's pale countenance. He was like a statue; not a tear came from his eyes. At length, with an almost convulsive movement of the right arm towards the corpse, he murmured hoarsely, "Did the stars compel you to make the son whom you loved miserable?" Throwing his hands behind his back and stepping a short pace backwards, the Baron raised his eyes upwards and said in a low and well-nigh broken voice, "Poor, infatuated old man! Your carnival farce with its shallow delusions is now over. Now you no doubt see that the possessions which are so niggardly dealt out to us here on earth have nothing in common with Hereafter beyond the stars. What will — what power can reach over beyond the grave?" The Baron was silent again for some seconds, then he cried passionately, "No, your perversity shall not rob me of a grain of my earthly happiness, which you strove so hard to destroy," and therewith he took a folded paper out of his pocket and held it up between two fingers to one of the burning candles that stood close beside the corpse. The paper was caught by the flame and blazed up high; and as the reflection flickered and played upon the face of the corpse, it was as though its muscles moved and as though the old man uttered toneless words, so that the servants who stood some distance off were filled with great horror and awe. The Baron calmly finished what he was doing by carefully stamping out with his foot the last fragment of paper that fell on the floor blazing. Then, casting yet another moody glance upon his father, he hurriedly left the hall.

On the following day Daniel reported to the Freiherr the damage that had been done to the tower, and described at great length all that had taken place on the night when their dear dead master died; and he concluded by saying that it would be a very wise thing to have the tower repaired at once, for, if a further fall were to take place, there would be some danger of the whole castle — well, if not tumbling down, at any rate suffering serious damage.

"Repair the tower?" the Freiherr interrupted the old servant curtly, whilst his eyes flashed with anger, "Repair the tower? Never, never! Don't you see, old man," he went on more calmly, "don't you see that the tower could not fall in this way without some special cause? How if it was my father's own wish that the place where he carried on his unhallowed astrological labours should be destroyed — how if he had himself made certain preparations by which he was enabled to bring down the turret whenever he pleased and so occasion the ruin of the interior of the tower! But be that as it may. And if the whole castle tumbles down, I shan't care; I shall be glad. Do you imagine I am going to dwell in this weird owls' nest? No; my wise ancestor who had the foundations of a new castle laid in the beautiful valley yonder — he has begun a work which I intend to finish." Daniel said crestfallen, "Then will all your faithful old servants have to take up their bundles and go?" "That I am not going to be waited upon by helpless, weak-kneed old fellows like you is quite certain; but for all that I shall turn none away. You may all enjoy the bread of charity without working for it." "And am I," cried the old man, greatly hurt, "am I, the house-steward, to be forced to lead such a life of inactivity?" Then the Freiherr, who had turned his back upon the old man and was about to leave the room, wheeled suddenly round, his face perfectly ablaze with passion, strode up to the old man as he stretched out his doubled fist towards him, and shouted in a thundering voice, "You, you hypocritical old villain, it's you who helped my old father in his unearthly practices up yonder; you lay upon his heart like a vampire; and perhaps it was you who basely took advantage of the old man's mad folly to plant in his mind those diabolical ideas which brought me to the brink of ruin. I ought, I tell you, to kick you out like a mangy cur." The old man was so terrified at these harsh terrible words that he threw himself upon his knees beside the Freiherr; but the Baron, as he spoke these last words, threw forward his right foot, perhaps quite unintentionally (as is frequently the case in anger, when the body mechanically obeys the mind, and what is in the thought is imitatively realised in action) and hit the old man so hard on the chest that he rolled over with a stifled scream. Rising painfully to his feet and uttering a most singular sound, like the howling whimper of an animal wounded to death, he looked the Freiherr through and through with a look that glared with mingled rage and despair. The purse of money which the Freiherr threw down as he went out of the room, the old man left lying on the floor where it fell.

Meanwhile all the nearest relatives of the family who lived in the neighbourhood had arrived, and the old Freiherr was interred with much pomp in the family vault in the church at R— sitten; and now, after the invited guests had departed, the new lord of the entail appeared to shake off his gloomy mood, and to be prepared to duly enjoy the property that had fallen to him. Along with V——, the old Freiherr's Justitiarius, who won his full confidence in the very first interview they had, and who was at once confirmed in his office, the Baron made an exact calculation of his sources of income, and considered how large a part he could devote to making improvements and how large a part to building a new castle. V—— was of opinion that the old Freiherr could not possibly have spent all his income every year, and that there must certainly be money concealed somewhere, since he had found nothing amongst his papers except one or two bank-notes for insignificant sums, and the ready-money in the iron safe was but very little more than a thousand thalers, or about £150. Who would be so likely to know anything about it as Daniel, who in his obstinate self-willed way was perhaps only waiting to be asked about it? The Baron was now not a little concerned at the thought that Daniel, whom he had so grossly insulted, might let large sums moulder somewhere sooner than discover them to him, not so much, of course, from any motives of self-interest,— for of what use could even the largest sum of money be to him, a childless old man, whose only wish was to end his days in the castle of R— sitten?— as from a desire to take vengeance for the affront put upon him. He gave V—— a circumstantial account of the entire scene with Daniel, and concluded by saying that from several items of information communicated to him he had learned that it was Daniel alone who had contrived to nourish in the old Freiherr's mind such an inexplicable aversion to ever seeing his sons in R— sitten. The Justitiarius declared that this information was perfectly false, since there was not a human creature on the face of the earth who would have been able to guide the Freiherr's thoughts in any way, far less determine them for him; and he undertook finally to draw from Daniel the secret, if he had one, as to the place in which they would be likely to find money concealed. His task proved far easier than he had anticipated, for no sooner did he begin, "But how comes it, Daniel, that your old master has left so little ready-money?" than Daniel replied, with a repulsive smile, "Do you mean the few trifling thalers, Herr Justitiarius, which you found in the little strong box? Oh! the rest is lying in the vault beside our gracious master's sleeping-cabinet. But the best," he went on to say, whilst his smile passed over into an abominable grin, and his eyes flashed with malicious fire, "but the best of all — several thousand gold pieces — lies buried at the bottom of the chasm beneath the ruins." The Justitiarius at once summoned the Freiherr; they proceeded there, and then into the sleeping-cabinet, where Daniel pushed aside the wainscot in one of the corners, and a small lock became visible. Whilst the Freiherr was regarding the polished lock with covetous eyes, and making preparations to try and unlock it with the keys of the great bunch which he dragged with some difficulty out of his pocket, Daniel drew himself up to his full height, and looked down with almost malignant pride upon his master, who had now stooped down in order to see the lock better. Daniel's face was deadly pale, and he said, his voice trembling, "If I am a dog, my lord Freiherr, I have also at least a dog's fidelity." Therewith he held out a bright steel key to his master, who greedily snatched it out of his hand, and with it he easily succeeded in opening the door. They stepped into a small and low-vaulted apartment, in which stood a large iron coffer with the lid open, containing many money-bags, upon which lay a strip of parchment, written in the old Freiherr's familiar handwriting, large and old-fashioned.

One hundred and fifty thousand Imperial thalers in old Fredericks d'or,8 money saved from the revenues of the estate-tail of R— sitten; this sum has been set aside for the building of the castle. Further, the lord of the entail who succeeds me in the possession of this money shall, upon the highest hill situated eastward from the old tower of the castle (which he will find in ruins), erect a high beacon tower for the benefit of mariners, and cause a fire to be kindled on it every night. R— sitten, on Michaelmas Eve of the year 1760. RODERICK, FREIHERR von R.

The Freiherr lifted up the bags one after the other and let them fall again into the coffer, delighted at the ringing clink of so much gold coin; then he turned round abruptly to the old house-steward, thanked him for the fidelity he had shown, and assured him that they were only vile tattling calumnies which had induced him to treat him so harshly in the first instance. He should not only remain in the castle, but should also continue to discharge his duties, uncurtailed in any way, as house-steward, and at double the wages he was then having. "I owe you a large compensation; if you will take money, help yourself to one of these bags." As he concluded with these words, the Baron stood before the old man, with his eyes bent upon the ground, and pointed to the coffer; then, approaching it again, he once more ran his eyes over the bags. A burning flush suddenly mounted into the old house-steward's cheeks, and he uttered that awful howling whimper — a noise as of an animal wounded to death, according to the Freiherr's previous description of it to the Justitiarius. The latter shuddered, for the words which the old man murmured between his teeth sounded like, "Blood for gold." Of all this the Freiherr, absorbed in the contemplation of the treasure before him, had heard not the least. Daniel tottered in every limb, as if shaken by an ague fit; approaching the Freiherr with bowed head in a humble attitude, he kissed his hand, and drawing his handkerchief across his eyes under the pretence of wiping away his tears, said in a whining voice, "Alas! my good and gracious master, what am I, a poor childless old man, to do with money? But the doubled wages I accept with gladness, and will continue to do my duty faithfully and zealously."

The Freiherr, who had paid no particular heed to the old man's words, now let the heavy lid of the coffer fall to with a bang, so that the whole room shook and cracked, and then, locking the coffer and carefully withdrawing the key, he said carelessly, "Very well, very well, old man." But after they entered the hall he went on talking to Daniel, "But you said something about a quantity of gold pieces buried underneath the ruins of the tower?" Silently the old man stepped towards the postern, and after some difficulty unlocked it. But so soon as he threw it open the storm drove a thick mass of snow-flakes into the hall; a raven was disturbed and flew in croaking and screaming and dashed with its black wings against the window, but regaining the open postern it disappeared downwards into the chasm. The Freiherr stepped out into the corridor; but one single glance downwards, and he started back trembling. "A fearful sight!— I'm giddy!" he stammered as he sank almost fainting into the Justitiarius' arms. But quickly recovering himself by an effort, he fixed a sharp look upon the old man and asked, "Down there, you say?" Meanwhile the old man had been locking the postern, and was now leaning against it with all his bodily strength, and was gasping and grunting to get the great key out of the rusty lock. This at last accomplished, he turned round to the Baron, and, changing the huge key about backwards and forwards in his hands, replied with a peculiar smile, "Yes, there are thousands and thousands down there — all my dear dead master's beautiful instruments — telescopes, quadrants, globes, dark mirrors, they all lie smashed to atoms underneath the ruins between the stones and the big balk." "But money — coined money," interrupted the Baron, "you spoke of gold pieces, old man?" "I only meant things which had cost several thousand gold pieces," he replied; and not another word could be got out of him.

The Baron appeared highly delighted to have all at once come into possession of all the means requisite for carrying out his favourite plan, namely, that of building a new and magnificent castle. The Justitiarius indeed stated it as his opinion that, according to the will of the deceased, the money could only be applied to the repair and complete finishing of the interior of the old castle, and further, any new erection would hardly succeed in equalling the commanding size and the severe and simple character of the old ancestral castle. The Freiherr, however, persisted in his intention, and maintained that in the disposal of property respecting which nothing was stated in the deeds of the entail the irregular will of the deceased could have no validity. He at the same time led V—— to understand that he should conceive it to be his duty to embellish R— sitten as far as the climate, soil, and environs would permit, for it was his intention to bring home shortly as his dearly loved wife a lady who was in every respect worthy of the greatest sacrifices.

The air of mystery with which the Freiherr spoke of this alliance, which possibly had been already consummated in secret, cut short all further questions from the side of the Justitiarius. Nevertheless he found in it to some extent a redeeming feature, for the Freiherr's eager grasping after riches now appeared to be due not so much to avarice strictly speaking as to the desire to make one dear to him forget the more beautiful country she was relinquishing for his sake. Otherwise he could not acquit the Baron of being avaricious, or at any rate insufferably close-fisted, seeing that, even though rolling in money and even when gloating over the old Fredericks d'or, he could not help bursting out with the peevish grumble, "I know the old rascal has concealed from us the greatest part of his wealth, but next spring I will have the ruins of the tower turned over under my own eyes."

The Freiherr had architects come, and discussed with them at great length what would be the most convenient way to proceed with his castle-building. He rejected one drawing after another; in none of them was the style of architecture sufficiently rich and grandiose. He now began to draw plans himself, and, inspirited by this employment, which constantly placed before his eyes a sunny picture of the happiest future, brought himself into such a genial humour that it often bordered on wild exuberance of spirits, and even communicated itself to all about him. His generosity and profuse hospitality belied all imputations of avarice at any rate. Daniel also seemed to have now forgotten the insult that had been put upon him. Towards the Freiherr, although often followed by him with mistrustful eyes on account of the treasure buried in the chasm, his bearing was both quiet and humble. But what struck everybody as extraordinary was that the old man appeared to grow younger from day to day. Possibly this might be, because he had begun to forget his grief for his old master, which had stricken him sore, and possibly also because he had not now, as he once had, to spend the cold nights in the tower without sleep, and got better food and good wine such as he liked; but whatever the cause might be, the old greybeard seemed to be growing into a vigorous man with red cheeks and well-nourished body, who could walk firmly and laugh loudly whenever he heard a jest to laugh at.

The pleasant tenor of life at R— sitten was disturbed by the arrival of a man whom one would have judged to be quite in his element there. This was Wolfgang's younger brother Hubert, at the sight of whom Wolfgang had screamed out, with his face as pale as a corpse's, "Unhappy wretch, what do you want here?" Hubert threw himself into his brother's arms, but Wolfgang took him and led him away up to a retired room, where he locked himself in with him. They remained closeted several hours, at the end of which time Hubert came down, greatly agitated, and called for his horses. The Justitiarius intercepted him; Hubert tried to pass him; but V——, inspired by the hope that he might perhaps stifle in the bud what might else end in a bitter life-long quarrel between the brothers, besought him to stay, at least a few hours, and at the same moment the Freiherr came down calling, "Stay here, Hubert! you will think better of it." Hubert's countenance cleared up; he assumed an air of composure, and quickly pulling off his costly fur coat, and throwing it to a servant behind him, he grasped V——'s hand and went with him into the room, saying with a scornful smile, "So the lord of the entail will tolerate my presence here, it seems." V—— thought that the unfortunate misunderstanding would assuredly be smoothed away now, for it was only separation and existence apart from each other that would, he conceived, be able to foster it. Hubert took up the steel tongs which stood near the fire-grate, and as he proceeded to break up a knotty piece of wood that would only sweal, not burn, and to rake the fire together better, he said to V——, "You see what a good-natured fellow I am, Herr Justitiarius, and that I am skilful in all domestic matters. But Wolfgang is full of the most extraordinary prejudices, and — a bit of a miser." V—— did not deem it advisable to attempt to fathom further the relations between the brothers, especially as Wolfgang's face and conduct and voice plainly showed that he was shaken to the very depths of his nature by diverse violent passions.

Late in the evening V—— had occasion to go up to the Freiherr's room in order to learn his decision about some matter or other connected with the estate-tail. He found him pacing up and down the room with long strides, his arms crossed on his back, and much perturbation in his manner. On perceiving the Justitiarius he stood still, and then, taking him by both hands and looking him gloomily in the face, he said in a broken voice, "My brother is come. I know what you are going to say," he proceeded almost before V—— had opened his mouth to put a question. "Unfortunately you know nothing. You don't know that my unfortunate brother — yes, I will not call him anything worse than unfortunate — that, like a spirit of evil, he crosses my path everywhere, ruining my peace of mind. It is not his fault that I have not been made unspeakably miserable; he did his best to make me so, but Heaven willed it otherwise. Ever since he has known of the conversion of the property into an entail, he has persecuted me with deadly hatred. He envies me this property, which in his hands would only be scattered like chaff. He is the wildest spendthrift I ever heard of. His load of debt exceeds by a long way the half of the unentailed property in Courland that fell to him, and now, pursued by his creditors, who fail not to worry him for payment, he hurries here to me to beg for money." "And you, his brother, refuse to give him any?" V—— was about to interrupt him; but the Freiherr, letting V——'s hands fall, and taking a long step backwards, went on in a loud and vehement tone. "Stop! yes; I refuse. I neither can nor will give away a single thaler of the revenues of the entail. But listen, and I will tell you what was the proposal which I made the insane fellow a few hours ago, and made in vain, and then pass judgment upon the feelings of duty by which I am actuated. Our unentailed possessions in Courland are, as you are aware, considerable; the half that falls to me I am willing to renounce, but in favour of his family. For Hubert has married, in Courland, a beautiful lady, but poor. She and the children she has borne him are starving. The estates should be put under trust; sufficient should be set aside out of the revenues to support him, and his creditors be paid by arrangement. But what does he care for a quiet life — a life free of anxiety?— what does he care for wife and child? Money, ready-money, and large quantities, is what he will have, that he may squander it in infamous folly. Some demon has made him acquainted with the secret of the hundred and fifty thousand thalers, half of which he in his mad way demands, maintaining that this money is movable property and quite apart from the entailed portion. This, however, I must and will refuse him, but the feeling haunts me that he is plotting my destruction in his heart."

No matter how great the efforts which V—— made to persuade the Freiherr out of this suspicion against his brother, in which, of course, not being initiated into the more circumstantial details of the disagreement, he could only appeal to broad and somewhat superficial moral principles, he yet could not boast of the smallest success. The Freiherr commissioned him to treat with his hostile and avaricious brother Hubert. V—— proceeded to do so with all the circumspection he was master of, and was not a little gratified when Hubert at length declared, "Be it so then; I will accept my brother's proposals, but upon condition that he will now, since I am on the point of losing both my honour and my good name for ever through the severity of my creditors, make me an advance of a thousand Fredericks d'or in hard cash, and further grant that in time to come I may take up my residence, at least for a short time occasionally, in our beautiful R— sitten, along with my good brother." "Never, never!" exclaimed the Freiherr violently, when V—— laid his brother's amended counter-proposals before him. "I will never consent that Hubert stay in my house even a single minute after I have brought home my wife. Go, my good friend, tell this mar-peace that he shall have two thousand Fredericks d'or, not as an advance, but as a gift — only, bid him go, bid him go." V—— now learned at one and the same time that the ground of the quarrel between the two brothers must be sought for in this marriage. Hubert listened to the Justitiarius proudly and calmly, and when he finished speaking replied in a hoarse and hollow tone, "I will think it over; but for the present I shall stay a few days in the castle." V—— exerted himself to prove to the discontented Hubert that the Freiherr, by making over his share of their unentailed property, was really doing all he possibly could do to indemnify him, and that on the whole he had no cause for complaint against his brother, although at the same time he admitted that all institutions of the nature of primogeniture, which vested such preponderant advantages in the eldest-born to the prejudice of the remaining children, were in many respects hateful. Hubert tore his waistcoat open from top to bottom like a man whose breast was cramped and he wanted to relieve it by fresh air. Thrusting one hand into his open shirt-frill and planting the other in his side, he spun round on one foot in a quick pirouette and cried in a sharp voice, "Pshaw! What is hateful is born of hatred." Then bursting out into a shrill fit of laughter, he said, "What condescension my lord of the entail shows in being thus willing to throw his gold pieces to the poor beggar!" V—— saw plainly that all idea of a complete reconciliation between the brothers was quite out of the question.

To the Freiherr's annoyance, Hubert established himself in the rooms that had been appointed for him in one of the side wings of the castle as if with the view to a very long stay. He was observed to hold frequent and long conversations with the house-steward; nay, the latter was sometimes even seen to accompany him when he went out wolf-hunting. Otherwise he was very little seen, and studiously avoided meeting his brother alone, at which the latter was very glad. V—— felt how strained and unpleasant this state of things was, and was obliged to confess to himself that the peculiar uneasiness which marked all that Hubert both said and did was such as to destroy intentionally and effectually all the pleasure of the place. He now perfectly understood why the Freiherr had manifested so much alarm on seeing his brother.

One day as V—— was sitting by himself in the justice-room amongst his law-papers, Hubert came in with a grave and more composed manner than usual, and said in a voice that bordered upon melancholy, "I will accept my brother's last proposals. If you will contrive that I have the two thousand Fredericks d'or today, I will leave the castle this very night — on horseback — alone." "With the money?"

asked V——. "You are right," replied Hubert; "I know what you would say — the weight! Give it me in bills on Isaac Lazarus of K——. For to K—— I am going this very night. Something is driving me away from this place. The old fellow has bewitched it with evil spirits." "Do you mean your father, Herr Baron?" asked V—— sternly. Hubert's lips trembled; he had to cling to the chair to keep from falling; but then suddenly recovering himself, he cried, "To-day then, please, Herr Justitiarius," and staggered to the door, not, however, without some exertion. "He now sees that no deceptions are any longer of avail, that he can do nothing against my firm will," said the Freiherr whilst drawing up the bills on Isaac Lazarus in K——. A burden was lifted off his heart by the departure of his inimical brother; and for a long time he had not been in such cheerful spirits as he was at supper. Hubert had sent his excuses; and there was not one who regretted his absence.

The room which V—— occupied was somewhat retired, and its windows looked upon the castle-yard. In the night he was suddenly startled up out of his sleep, and was under the impression that he had been awakened by a distant and pitiable moan. But listen as he would, all remained still as the grave, and so he was obliged to conclude that the sound which had fallen upon his ears was the delusion of a dream. But at the same time he was seized with such a peculiar feeling of breathless anxiety and terror that he could not stay in bed. He got up and approached the window. It was not long, however, before the castle door was opened, and a figure with a blazing torch came out of the castle and went across the court-yard. V—— recognised the figure as that of old Daniel, and saw him open the stable-door and go in, and soon afterwards bring out a saddle horse. Now a second figure came into view out of the darkness, well wrapped in furs, and with a fox-skin cap on his head. V—— perceived that it was Hubert; but after he had spoken excitedly with Daniel for some minutes, he returned into the castle. Daniel led back the horse into the stable and locked the door, and also that of the castle, after he had returned across the court-yard in the same way in which he crossed it before. It was evident Hubert had intended to go away on horseback, but had suddenly changed his mind; and no less evident was it that there was a dangerous understanding of some sort between Hubert and the old house-steward. V—— looked forward to the morning with burning impatience; he would acquaint the Freiherr with the occurrences of the night. Really it was now time to take precautionary measures against the attacks of Hubert's malice, which V—— was now convinced, had been betrayed in his agitated behaviour of the day before.

Next morning, at the hour when the Freiherr was in the habit of rising, V—— heard people running backwards and forwards, doors opened and slammed to, and a tumultuous confusion of voices talking and shouting. On going out of his room he met servants everywhere, who, without heeding him, ran past him with ghastly pale faces, upstairs, downstairs, in and out the rooms. At length he ascertained that the Freiherr was missing, and that they had been looking for him for hours in vain. As he had gone to bed in the presence of his personal attendant, he must have afterwards got up and gone away somewhere in his dressing-gown and slippers, taking the large candlestick with him, for these articles were also missed. V——, his mind agitated with dark forebodings, ran up to the ill-fated hall, the cabinet adjoining which Wolfgang had chosen, like his father, for his own bedroom. The postern leading to the tower stood wide open, with a cry of horror V—— shouted, "There — he lies dashed to pieces at the bottom of the ravine." And it was so. There had been a fall of snow, so that all they could distinctly make out from above was the rigid arm of the unfortunate man protruding from between the stones. Many hours passed before the workmen succeeded, at great risk of life, in descending by means of ladders bound together, and drawing up the corpse by the aid of ropes. In the last agonies of death the Baron had kept a tight hold upon the silver candlestick; the hand in which it was clenched was the only uninjured part of his whole body, which had been shattered in the most hideous way by rebounding on the sharp stones.

Just as the corpse was drawn up and carried into the hall, and laid upon the very same spot on the large table where a few weeks before old Roderick had lain dead, Hubert burst in, his face distorted by the frenzy of despair. Quite overpowered by the fearful sight he wailed, "Brother! O my poor brother! No; this I never prayed for from the demons who had entered into me." This suspicious self-exculpation made V—— tremble; he felt impelled to proceed against

Hubert as the murderer of his brother. Hubert, however, had fallen on the floor senseless; they carried him to bed; but on taking strong restoratives he soon recovered. Then he appeared in V——'s room, pale and sorrow-stricken, and with his eyes half clouded with grief; and unable to stand owing to his weakness, he slowly sank down into an easy-chair, saying, "I have wished for my brother's death, because my father had made over to him the best part of the property through the foolish conversion of it into an entail. He has now found a fearful death. I am now lord of the estate-tail, but my heart is rent with pain — I can — I shall never be happy. I confirm you in your office; you shall be invested with the most extensive powers in respect to the management of the estate, upon which I cannot bear to live." Hubert left the room, and in two or three hours was on his way to K——.

It appeared that the unfortunate Wolfgang had got up in the night, probably with the intention of going into the other cabinet where there was a library. In the stupor of sleep he had mistaken the door, and had opened the postern, taken a step out, and plunged headlong down. But after all had been said, there was nevertheless a good deal that was strained and unlikely in this explanation. If the Baron was unable to sleep and wanted to get a book out of the library, this of itself excluded all idea of sleep-stupor; but this condition alone could account for any mistaking of the postern for the door of the cabinet. Then again, the former was fast locked, and required a good deal of exertion to unlock it. These improbabilities V—— accordingly put before the domestics, who had gathered round him, and at length the Freiherr's body-servant, Francis by name, said, "Nay, nay, my good Herr Justitiarius; it couldn't have happened in that way." "Well, how then?" asked V—— abruptly and sharply. But Francis, a faithful, honest fellow, who would have followed his master into his grave, was unwilling to speak out before the rest; he stipulated that what he had to say about the event should be confided to the Justitiarius alone in private. V—— now learned that the Freiherr used often to talk to Francis about the vast treasure which he believed lay buried beneath the ruins of the tower, and also that frequently at night, as if goaded by some malicious fiend, he would open the postern, the key of which Daniel had been obliged to give him, and would gaze with longing eyes down into the chasm where the supposed riches lay. There was now no doubt about it; on that ill-omened night the Freiherr, after his servant had left him, must have taken one of his usual walks to the postern, where he had been most likely suddenly seized with dizziness, and had fallen over. Daniel, who also seemed much upset by the Freiherr's terrible end, thought it would be a good thing to have the dangerous postern walled up; and this was at once done.

Freiherr Hubert von R——, who had then succeeded to the entail, went back to Courland without once showing himself at R— sitten again. V—— was invested with full powers for the absolute management of the property. The building of the new castle was not proceeded with; but on the other hand the old structure was put in as good a state of repair as possible. Several years passed before Hubert came again to R— sitten, late in the autumn, but after he had remained shut up in his room with V—— for several days, he went back to Courland. Passing on his way through K——, he deposited his will with the government authorities there.

The Freiherr, whose character appeared to have undergone a complete revolution, spoke more than once during his stay at R— sitten of presentiments of his approaching death. And these apprehensions were really not unfounded, for he died in the very next year. His son, named, like the deceased Baron, Hubert, soon came over from Courland to take possession of the rich inheritance; and was followed by his mother and his sister. The youth seemed to unite in his own person all the bad qualities of his ancestors: he proved himself to be proud, arrogant, impetuous, avaricious, in the very first moments after his arrival at R— sitten. He wanted to have several things which did not suit his notions of what was right and proper altered there and then: the cook he kicked out of doors; and he attempted to thrash the coachman, in which, however, he did not succeed, for the big brawny fellow had the impudence not to submit to it. In fact, he was on the high road to assuming the rôle of a harsh and severe lord of the entail, when V—— interposed in his firm earnest manner, declaring most explicitly that not a single chair should be moved, that not even a cat should leave the house if she liked to stay in it, until after the will had been opened. "You have the presumption to tell me, the lord of the entail," began the Baron. V——, however, cut short the young man, who was foaming with rage, and said, whilst he measured him with a keen searching glance, "Don't be in too great a hurry, Herr Baron. At all events, you have no right to exercise authority here until after the opening of your father's will. It is I— I alone — who am now master here; and I shall know how to meet violence with violent measures. Please to recollect that by virtue of my powers as executor of your father's will, as well as by virtue of the arrangements which have been made by the court, I am empowered to forbid your remaining in R— sitten if I think fit to do so; and so, if you wish to spare me this disagreeable step, I would advise you to go away quietly to K——." The lawyer's earnestness, and the resolute tone in which he spoke, lent the proper emphasis to his words. Hence the young Baron, who was charging with far two sharp-pointed horns, felt the weakness of his weapons against the firm bulwark, and found it convenient to cover the shame of his retreat with a burst of scornful laughter.

Three months passed and the day was come on which, in accordance with the expressed wish of the deceased, his will was to be opened at K——, where it had been deposited. In the chambers there was, besides the officers of the court, the Baron, and V——, a young man of noble appearance, whom V—— had brought with him, and who was taken to be V——'s clerk, since he had a parchment deed sticking out from the breast of his buttoned-up coat. Him the Baron treated as he did nearly all the rest, with scornful contempt; and he demanded with noisy impetuosity that they should make haste and get done with all their tiresome needless ceremonies as quickly as possible and without over many words and scribblings. He couldn't for the life of him make out why any will should be wanted at all with respect to the inheritance, and especially in the case of entailed property; and no matter what provisions were made in the will, it would depend entirely upon his decision as to whether they should be observed or not. After casting a hasty and surly glance at the handwriting and the seal, the Baron acknowledged them to be those of his dead father. Upon the clerk of the court preparing to read the will aloud, the young Baron, throwing his right arm carelessly over the back of his chair and leaning his left on the table, whilst he drummed with his fingers on its green cover, sat staring with an air of indifference out of the window. After a short preamble the deceased Freiherr Hubert von R—— declared that he had never possessed the estate-tail as its lawful owner, but that he had only managed it in the name of the deceased Freiherr Wolfgang von R—— 's only son, called Roderick after his grandfather; and he it was to whom, according to the rights of family priority, the estate had fallen on his father's death. Amongst Hubert's papers would be found an exact account of all revenues and expenditure, as well as of existing movable property, &c. The will went on to relate that Wolfgang von R—— had, during his travels, made the acquaintance of Mdlle. Julia de St. Val in Geneva, and had fallen so deeply in love with her that he resolved never to leave her side again. She was very poor; and her family, although noble and of good repute, did not, however, rank amongst the most illustrious, for which

96

reason Wolfgang dared not expect to receive the consent of old Roderick to a union with her, for the old Freiherr's aim and ambition was to promote by all possible means the establishment of a powerful family. Nevertheless he ventured to write from Paris to his father, acquainting him with the fact that his affections were engaged. But what he had foreseen was actually realised; the old Baron declared categorically that he had himself chosen the future mistress of the entail, and therefore there could never be any mention made of any other. Wolfgang, instead of crossing the Channel into England, as he was to have done, returned into Geneva under the assumed name of Born, and married Julia, who after the lapse of a year bore him a son, and this son became on Wolfgang's death the real lord of the entail. In explanation of the facts why Hubert, though acquainted with all this, had kept silent so long and had represented himself as lord of the entail, various reasons were assigned, based upon agreements formerly made with Wolfgang, but they seemed for the most part insufficient and devoid of real foundation.

The Baron sat staring at the clerk of the court as if thunderstruck, whilst the latter went on proclaiming all this bad news in a provokingly monotonous and jarring tone. When he finished, V—— rose, and taking the young man whom he had brought with him by the hand, said, as he bowed to the assembled company, "Here I have the honour to present to you, gentlemen, Freiherr Roderick von R——, lord of the entail of R— sitten." Baron Hubert looked at the youth, who had, as it were, fallen from the clouds to deprive him of the rich inheritance together with half the unentailed Courland estates, with suppressed fury in his gleaming eyes; then, threatening him with his doubled fist, he ran out of the court without uttering a word. Baron Roderick, on being challenged by the court-officers, produced the documents by which he was to establish his identity as the person whom he represented himself to be. He handed in an attested extract from the register of the church where his father was married, which certified that on such and such a day Wolfgang Born, merchant, born in K——, had been united in marriage with the blessing of the Church to Mdlle. Julia de St. Val, in the presence of certain witnesses, who were named. Further, he produced his own baptismal certificate (he had been baptized in Geneva as the son of the merchant Born and his wife Julia, née De St. Val, begotten in lawful wedlock), and various letters from his father to his mother, who was long since dead, but they none of them had any other signature than W.

V—— looked through all these papers with a cloud upon his face; and as he put them together again, he said, somewhat troubled, "Ah well! God will help us!"

The very next morning Freiherr Hubert von R—— presented, through an advocate whose services he had succeeded in enlisting in his cause, a statement of protest to the government authorities in K——, actually calling upon them to effectuate the immediate surrender to him of the entail of R— sitten. It was incontestable, maintained the advocate, that the deceased Freiherr Hubert Von R—— had not had the power to dispose of entailed property either by testament or in any other way. The testament in question, therefore, was nothing more than an evidential statement, written down and deposited with the court, to the effect that Freiherr Wolfgang von R—— had bequeathed the estate-tail to a son who was at that time still living; and accordingly it had as evidence no greater weight than that of any other witness, and so could not by any possibility legitimately establish the claims of the person who had announced himself to be Freiherr Roderick von R——. Hence it was rather the duty of this new claimant to prove by action at law his alleged rights of inheritance, which were hereby expressly disputed and denied, and so also to take proper steps to maintain his claim to the estate-tail, which now, according to the laws of succession, fell to Baron Hubert von R——. By the father's death the property came at once immediately into the hands of the son. There was no need for any formal declaration to be made of his entering into possession of the inheritance, since the succession could not be alienated; at any rate, the present owner of the estate was not going to be disturbed in his possession by claims which were perfectly groundless. Whatever reasons the deceased might have had for bringing forward another heir of entail were quite irrelevant. And it might be remarked that he had himself had an intrigue in Switzerland, as could be proved if necessary from the papers he had left behind him; and it was quite possible that the person whom he alleged to be his brother's son was his own son, the fruit of an unlawful love, for whom in a momentary fit of remorse he had wished to secure the entail.

However great was the balance of probability in favour of the truth of the circumstances as stated in the will, and however revolted the judges were, particularly by the last clauses of the protest, in which the son felt no compunction at accusing his dead father of a crime, yet the views of the case there stated were after all the right ones; and it was only due to V——'s restless exertions, and his explicit and solemn assurance that the proofs which were necessary to establish legitimately the identity of Freiherr Roderick von R—— should be produced in a very short time, that the surrender of the estate to the young Baron was deferred, and the contrivance of the administration of it in trust agreed to, until after the case should be settled.

V—— was only too well aware how difficult it would be for him to keep his promise. He had turned over all old Roderick's papers without finding the slightest trace of a letter or any kind of a statement bearing upon Wolfgang's relation to Mdlle. de St. Val. He was sitting wrapt in thought in old Roderick's sleeping-cabinet, every hole and corner of which he had searched, and was working at a long statement of the case that he intended despatching to a certain notary in Geneva, who had been recommended to him as a shrewd and energetic man, to request him to procure and forward certain documents which would establish the young Freiherr's cause on firm ground. It was midnight; the full moon shone in through the windows of the adjoining hall, the door of which stood open. Then V—— fancied he heard a noise as of some one coming slowly and heavily up the stairs, and also at the same time a jingling and rattling of keys. His attention was arrested; he rose to his feet and went into the hall, where he plainly made out that there was some one crossing the ante-room and approaching the door of the hall where he was. Soon afterwards the door was opened and a man came slowly in, dressed in night-clothes, his face ghastly pale and distorted; in the one hand he bore a candle-stick with the candles burning, and in the other a huge bunch of keys. V—— at once recognised the house-steward, and was on the point of addressing him and inquiring what he wanted so late at night, when he was arrested by an icy shiver; there was something so unearthly and ghost-like in the old man's manner and bearing as well as in his set, pallid face. He perceived that he was in presence of a somnambulist. Crossing the hall obliquely with measured strides, the old man went straight to the walled-up postern that had formerly led to the tower. He came to a halt immediately in front of it, and uttered a wailing sound that seemed to come from the bottom of his heart, and was so awful and so loud that the whole apartment rang again, making V—— tremble with dread. Then, setting the candlestick down on the floor and hanging the keys on his belt, Daniel began to scratch at the wall with both hands, so that the blood soon burst out from beneath his finger-nails, and all the while he was moaning and groaning as if tortured by nameless agony. After placing his ear against the wall in a listening attitude, he waved his hand as if hushing some one, stooped down and picked up the candlestick, and finally stole back to the door with soft measured footsteps. V—— took his own candle in his hand and cautiously followed him. They both went downstairs; the old man unlocked the great main door of the castle, V—— slipped cleverly through. Then they went to the stable, where old Daniel, to V——'s perfect astonishment, placed his candlestick so skilfully that the entire interior of the building was sufficiently lighted without the least danger. Having fetched a saddle and bridle, he put them on one of the horses which he had loosed from the manger, carefully tightening the girth and taking up the stirrup-straps. Pulling the tuft of hair on the horse's forehead outside the front strap, he took him by the bridle and led him out of the stable, clicking with his tongue and patting his neck with one hand. On getting outside in the courtyard he stood several seconds in the attitude of one receiving commands, which he promised by sundry nods to carry out. Then he led the horse back into the stable, unsaddled him, and tied him to the manger. This done, he took his candlestick, locked the stable, and returned to the castle, finally disappearing in his own room, the door of which he carefully bolted. V—— was deeply agitated by this scene; the presentiment of some fearful deed rose up before him like a black and fiendish spectre, and refused to leave him. Being so keenly alive as he was to the precarious position of his protégé, he felt that it would at least be his duty to turn what he had seen to his account.

Next day, just as it was beginning to be dusk, Daniel came into the Justitiarius's room to receive some instructions relating to his department of the household. V—— took him by the arms, and forcing him into a chair, in a confidential way began, "See you here, my old friend Daniel, I have long been wishing to ask you what you think of all this confused mess into which Hubert's peculiar will has tumbled us. Do you really think that the young man is Wolfgang's son, begotten in lawful marriage?" The old man, leaning over the arm of his chair, and avoiding V——'s eyes, for V—— was watching him most intently, replied doggedly, "Bah! Maybe he is; maybe he is not. What does it matter to me? It's all the same to me who's master here now." "But I believe," went on V——, moving nearer to the old man and placing his hand on his shoulder, "but I believed you possessed the old Freiherr's full confidence, and in that case he assuredly would not conceal from you the real state of affairs with regard to his sons. He told you, I dare say, about the marriage which Wolfgang had made against his will, did he not?" "I don't remember to have ever heard him say anything of that sort," replied the old man, yawning with the most ill-mannered loudness. "You are sleepy, old man," said V——; "perhaps you have had a restless night?" "Not that I am aware," he rejoined coldly; "but I must go and order supper." Whereupon he rose heavily from his chair and rubbed his bent back, yawning again, and that still more loudly than before. "Stay a little while, old man," cried V——, taking hold of his hand and endeavouring to force him to resume his seat; but Daniel preferred to stand in front of the study-table; propping himself upon it with both hands, and leaning across towards

103

V——, he asked sullenly, "Well, what do you want? What have I to do with the will? What do I care about the quarrel over the estate?" "Well, well," interposed V——, "we'll say no more about that now. Let us turn to some other topic, Daniel. You are out of humour and yawning, and all that is a sign of great weariness, and I am almost inclined to believe that it really was you last night, who"—— "Well, what did I do last night?" asked the old man without changing his position. V—— went on, "Last night, when I was sitting up above in your old master's sleeping-cabinet next the great hall, you came in at the door, your face pale and rigid; and you went across to the bricked-up postern and scratched at the wall with both your hands, groaning as if in very great pain. Do you walk in your sleep, Daniel?" The old man dropped back into the chair which V—— quickly managed to place for him; but not a sound escaped his lips. His face could not be seen, owing to the gathering dusk of the evening; V—— only noticed that he took his breath short and that his teeth were rattling together. "Yes," continued V—— after a short pause, "there is one thing that is very strange about sleep-walkers. On the day after they have been in this peculiar state in which they have acted as if they were perfectly wide awake, they don't remember the least thing, that they did." Daniel did not move. "I have come across something like what your condition was yesterday once before in the course of my experience," proceeded V——. "I had a friend who regularly began to wander about at night as you do whenever it was full moon,— nay, he often sat down and wrote letters. But what was most extraordinary was that if I began to whisper softly in his ear I could soon manage to make him speak; and he would answer correctly all the questions I put to him; and even things that he would most jealously have concealed when awake now fell from his lips unbidden, as though he were unable to offer any resistance to the power that was exerting its influence over him. Deuce take it! I really believe that, if a man who's given to walking in his sleep had ever committed any crime, and hoarded it up as a secret ever so long, it could be extracted from him by questioning when he was in this peculiar state. Happy are they who have a clean conscience like you and me, Daniel! We may walk as much as we like in our sleep; there's no fear of anybody extorting the confession of a crime from us. But come now, Daniel! when you scratch so hideously at the bricked-up postern, you want, I dare say, to go up the astronomical tower, don't you? I suppose you want to go and experiment like old Roderick — eh? Well, next time you come, I shall ask you what you want to do." Whilst V—— was speaking, the old man was shaken with continually increasing agitation; but now his whole frame seemed to heave and rock convulsively past all hope of cure, and in a shrill voice he began to utter a string of unmeaning gibberish. V—— rang for the servants. They brought lights; but as the old man's fit did not abate, they lifted him up as though he had been a mere automaton, not possessed of the power of voluntary movement, and carried him to bed. After continuing in this frightful state for about an hour, he fell into a profound sleep resembling a dead faint

When he awoke he asked for wine; and, after he had got what he wanted, he sent away the man who was going to sit with him, and locked himself in his room as usual.

V—— had indeed really resolved to make the attempt he spoke of to Daniel, although at the same time he could not forget two facts. In the first place, Daniel, having now been made aware of his propensity to walk in his sleep, would probably adopt every measure of precaution to avoid him; and on the other hand, confessions made whilst in this condition would not be exactly fitted to serve as a basis for further proceedings. In spite of this, however, he repaired to the hall on the approach of midnight, hoping that Daniel, as frequently happens to those afflicted in this way, would be constrained to act involuntarily. About midnight there arose a great noise in the courtyard. V—— plainly heard a window broken in; then he went downstairs, and as he traversed the passages he was met by rolling clouds of suffocating smoke, which, he soon perceived were pouring out of the open door of the house-steward's room. The steward himself was just being carried out, to all appearance dead, in order to be taken and put to bed in another room. The servants related that about midnight one of the under-grooms had been awakened by a strange hollow knocking; he thought something had befallen the old man, and was preparing to get up and go and see if he could help him, when the night watchman in the court shouted, "Fire! Fire! The Herr House–Steward's room is all of a bright blaze!" At this outcry several servants at once appeared on the scene; but all their efforts to burst open the room door were unavailing. Whereupon they hurried out into the court, but the resolute watchman had already broken in the window, for the room was low and on the basement story, had torn down the burning curtains, and by pouring a few buckets of water on them had at once extinguished the fire. The house-steward they found lying on the floor in the middle of the room in a swoon. In his hand he still held the candlestick tightly clenched, the burning candles of which had caught the curtains, and so occasioned the fire. Some of the blazing rags had fallen upon the old man, burning his eyebrows and a large portion of the hair of his head. If the watchman had not seen the fire the old man must have been helplessly burned to death. The servants, moreover, to their no little astonishment found the room door secured on the inside by two quite new bolts, which had been fastened on since the previous evening, for they had not been there then. V—— perceived that the old man had wished to make it impossible for him to get out of his room; for the blind impulse which urged him to wander in his sleep he could not resist. The old man became seriously ill; he did not speak; he took but little nourishment; and lay staring before him with the reflection of death in his set eyes, just as if he were clasped in the vice-like grip of some hideous thought. V—— believed he would never rise from his bed again.

V—— had done all that could be done for his client; and he could now only await the result in patience; and so he resolved to return to K——. His departure was fixed for the following morning. As he was packing his papers together late at night, he happened to lay his hand upon a little sealed packet which Freiherr Hubert von R—— had given him, bearing the inscription, "To be read after my will has been opened," and which by some unaccountable means had hitherto escaped his notice. He was on the point of breaking the seal when the door opened and Daniel came in with still, ghostlike step. Placing upon the table a black portfolio which he carried under his arm, he sank upon his knees with a deep groan, and grasping V——'s hands with a convulsive clutch he said, in a voice so hollow and hoarse that it seemed to come from the bottom of a grave, "I should not like to die on the scaffold! There is One above who judges!" Then, rising with some trouble and with many painful gasps, he left the room as he had come.

V—— spent the whole of the night in reading what the black portfolio and Hubert's packet contained. Both agreed in all circumstantial particulars, and suggested naturally what further steps were to be taken. On arriving at K——, V—— immediately repaired to Freiherr Hubert von R——, who received him with ill-mannered pride. But the remarkable result of the interview, which began at noon and lasted on without interruption until late at night, was that the next day the Freiherr made a declaration before the court to the effect that he acknowledged the claimant to be, agreeably to his father's will, the son of Wolfgang von R——, eldest son of Freiherr Roderick von R——, and begotten in lawful wedlock with Mdlle. Julia de St. Val, and furthermore acknowledged him as rightful and legitimate heir to the entail. On leaving the court he found his carriage, with post-horses, standing before the door; he stepped in and was driven off at a rapid rate, leaving his mother and his sister behind him. They would perhaps never see him again, he wrote, along with other perplexing statements. Roderick's astonishment at this unexpected turn which the case had taken was very great; he pressed V—— to explain to him how this wonder had been brought about, what mysterious power was at work in the matter. V——, however, evaded his questions by giving him hopes of telling him all at some future time, and when he should have come into possession of the estate. For the surrender of the entail to him could not be effected immediately, since the court, not content with Hubert's declaration, required that Roderick should also first prove his own identity to their satisfaction. V—— proposed to the Baron that he should go and live at R— sitten, adding that Hubert's mother and sister, momentarily embarrassed by his sudden departure, would prefer to go and live quietly on the ancestral property rather than stay in the dear and noisy town. The glad delight with which Roderick welcomed the prospect of dwelling, at least for a time, under the same roof with the Baroness and her daughter, betrayed the deep impression which the lovely and graceful Seraphina had made upon him. In fact, the Freiherr made such good use of his time in R— sitten that, at the end of a few weeks, he had won Seraphina's love as well as her mother's cordial approval of her marriage with him. All this was for V—— rather too quick work, since Roderick's claims to be lord of the entail still continued to be rather doubtful. The life of idyllic happiness at the castle was interrupted by letters from Courland. Hubert had not shown himself at all at the estates, but had travelled direct to St Petersburg, where he had taken military service and was now in the field against the Persians, with whom Russia happened to be just then waging war. This obliged the Baroness and her daughter to set off immediately for their Courland estates, where everything was in confusion and disorder. Roderick, who regarded himself in the light of an accepted son-inlaw, insisted upon accompanying his beloved; and hence, since V—— likewise returned to K——, the castle was left in its previous loneliness. The house-steward's malignant complaint grew worse and worse, so that he gave up all hopes of ever getting about again; and his office was conferred upon an old chasseur, Francis by name, Wolfgang's faithful servant.

At last, after long waiting, V—— received from Switzerland information of the most favourable character. The priest who had married Roderick was long since dead; but there was found in the church register a memorandum in his hand writing, to the effect that the man of the name of Born, whom he had joined in the bonds of wedlock with Mdlle. Julia de St. Val, had established completely to his satisfaction his identity as Freiherr Wolfgang von R——, eldest son of Freiherr Roderick von R—— of R— Sitten. Besides this, two witnesses of the marriage had been discovered, a merchant of Geneva and an old French captain, who had moved to Lyons; to them also Wolfgang had in confidence stated

110

his real name; and their affidavits confirmed the priest's notice in the church register. With these memoranda in his hands, drawn up with proper legal formalities, V—— now succeeded in securing his client in the complete possession of his rights; and as there was now no longer any hindrance to the surrender to him of the entail, it was to be put into his hands in the ensuing autumn. Hubert had fallen in his very first engagement, thus sharing the fate of his younger brother, who had likewise been slain in battle a year before his father's death. Thus the Courland estates fell to Baroness Seraphina von R——, and made a handsome dowry for her to take to the too happy Roderick.

November had already come in when the Baroness, along with Roderick and his betrothed, arrived at R— sitten. The formal surrender of the estate-tail to the young Baron took place, and then his marriage with Seraphina was solemnised. Many weeks passed amid a continual whirl of pleasure; but at length the wearied guests began gradually to depart from the castle, to V——'s great satisfaction, for he had made up his mind not to take his leave of R— sitten until he had initiated the young lord of the entail in all the relations and duties connected with his new position down to the minutest particulars. Roderick's uncle had kept an account of all revenues and disbursements with the most detailed accuracy; hence, since Hubert had only retained a small sum annually for his own support, the surplus revenues had all gone to swell the capital left by the old Freiherr, till the total now amounted to a considerable sum. Hubert had only employed the income of the entail for his own purposes during the first three years, but to cover this he had given a mortgage on the security of his share of the Courland property.

From the time when old Daniel had revealed himself to V—— as a somnambulist, V—— had chosen old Roderick's bed-room for his own sitting-room, in order that he might the more securely gather from the old man what he afterwards voluntarily disclosed. Hence it was in this room and in the adjoining great hall that the Freiherr transacted business with V——. Once they were both sitting at the great table by the bright blazing fire; V—— had his pen in his hand, and was noting down various totals and calculating the riches of the lord of the entail, whilst the latter, leaning his head on his hand, was blinking at the open account-books and formidable-looking documents. Neither of them heard the hollow roar of the sea, nor the anxious cries of the sea-gulls as they dashed against the windowpanes, flapping their wings and flying backwards and forwards, announcing the oncoming storm. Neither of them heeded the storm, which arose about midnight, and was now roaring and raging with wild fury round the castle walls, so that all the sounds of ill omen in the fire-grates and narrow passages awoke, and began to whistle and shriek in a weird, unearthly way. At length, after a terrific blast, which made the whole castle shake, the hall was completely lit up by the murky glare of the full moon, and V—— exclaimed, "Awful weather!" The Freiherr, quite absorbed in the consideration of the wealth which had fallen to him, replied indifferently, as he turned over a page of the receipt-book with a satisfied smile, "It is indeed; very stormy!" But, as if clutched by the icy hand of Dread, he started to his feet as the door of the hall flew open and a pale spectral figure became visible, striding in with the stamp of death upon its face. It was Daniel, who, lying helpless under the power of disease, was deemed in the opinion of V—— as of everybody else incapable of the ability to move a single limb; but, again coming under the influence of his propensity to wander in his sleep at full moon, he had, it appeared, been unable to resist it. The Freiherr stared at the old man without uttering a sound; and when Daniel began to scratch at the wall, and moan as though in the painful agonies of death, Roderick's heart was filled with horrible dread. With his face ashy pale and his hair standing straight on end, he leapt to his feet and strode towards the old man in a threatening attitude and cried in a loud firm voice, so that the hall rang again, "Daniel, Daniel, what are you doing here at this hour?" Then the old man uttered that same unearthly howling whimper, like the death-cry of a wounded animal, which he had uttered when Wolfgang had offered to reward his fidelity with gold; and he fell down on the floor. V—— summoned the servants; they raised the old man up; but all attempts to restore animation proved fruitless. Then the Freiherr cried, almost beside himself, "Good God! Good God! Now I remember to have heard that a sleepwalker may die on the spot if anybody calls him by his name. Oh! oh! unfortunate wretch that I am! I have killed the poor old man! I shall never more have a peaceful moment so long as

I live." When the servants had carried the corpse away and the hall was again empty, V—— took the Freiherr, who was still continuing his self-reproaches, by the hand and led him in impressive silence to the walled-up postern, and said, "The man who fell down dead at your feet, Freiherr Roderick, was the atrocious murderer of your father." The Freiherr fixed his staring eyes upon V—— as though he saw the foul fiends of hell. But V—— went on, "The time has come now for me to reveal to you the hideous secret which, weighing upon the conscience of this monster and burthening him with curses, compelled him to roam abroad in his sleep. The Eternal Power has seen fit to make the son take vengeance upon the murderer of his father. The words which you thundered in the ears of that fearful night-walker were the last words which your unhappy father spoke." V—— sat down in front of the fire, and the Freiherr, trembling and unable to utter a word, took his seat beside him. V—— began to tell him the contents of the document which Hubert had left behind him, and the seal of which he (V——) was not to break until after the opening of the will Hubert lamented, in expressions testifying to the deepest remorse, the implacable hatred against his elder brother which took root in him from the moment that old Roderick established the entail. He was deprived of all weapons; for, even if he succeeded in maliciously setting the son at variance with the father, it would serve no purpose, since even Roderick himself had not the power to deprive his eldest son of his birth-right, nor would he on principle have ever done so, no matter how his affections had been alienated from him. It was only when Wolfgang formed his connection with Julia de St. Val in Geneva that Hubert saw his way to effecting his brother's ruin. And that was the time when he came to an understanding with Daniel, to provoke the old man by villainous devices to take measures which should drive his son to despair.

He was well aware of old Roderick's opinion that the only way to ensure an illustrious future for the family to all subsequent time was by means of an alliance with one of the oldest families in the country. The old man had read this alliance in the stars, and any pernicious derangement of the constellation would only entail destruction upon the family he had founded. In this way it was that Wolfgang's union with Julia seemed to the old man like a sinful crime, committed against the ordinances of the Power which had stood by him in all his worldly undertakings; and any means that might be employed for Julia's ruin he would have regarded as justified for the same reason, for Julia had, he conceived, ranged herself against him like some demoniacal principle. Hubert knew that his brother loved Julia passionately, almost to madness in fact, and that the loss of her would infallibly make him miserable, perhaps kill him. And Hubert was all the more ready to assist the old man in his plans as he had himself conceived an unlawful affection for Julia, and hoped to win her for himself. It was, however, determined by a special dispensation of Providence that all attacks, even the most virulent, were to be thwarted by Wolfgang's resoluteness; nay, that he should contrive to deceive his brother: the fact that his marriage was actually solemnised and that of the birth of a son were kept secret from Hubert In Roderick's mind also there occurred, along with the presentiment of his approaching death, the idea that Wolfgang had really married the Julia who was so hostile to him. In the letter which commanded his son to appear at R— sitten on a given day to take possession of the entail, he cursed him if he did not sever his connection with her. This was the letter that Wolfgang burnt beside his father's corpse. To Hubert the old man wrote, saying that Wolfgang had married Julia, but that he would part from her. This Hubert took to be a fancy of his visionary father's; accordingly he was not a little dismayed when on reaching R— sitten Wolfgang with perfect frankness not only confirmed the old man's supposition, but also went on to add that Julia had borne him a son, and that he hoped in a short time to surprise her with the pleasant intelligence of his high rank and great wealth, for she had hitherto taken him for Born, a merchant from M———. He intended going to Geneva himself to fetch his beloved wife. But before he could carry out this plan he was overtaken by death. Hubert carefully concealed what he knew about the existence of a son born to Wolfgang in lawful wedlock with Julia, and so usurped the property that really belonged to his nephew. But only a few years passed before he became a prey to bitter remorse. He was reminded of his guilt in terrible wise by destiny, in the hatred which grew up and developed more and more between his two sons. "You are a poor starving beggar!" said the elder, a boy of twelve, to the younger, "but I shall be lord of R— sitten when father dies, and then you will have to be humble and kiss my hand when you want me to give you money to buy a new coat." The younger, goaded to ungovernable fury by his brother's proud and scornful words, threw the knife at him which he happened to have in his hand, and almost killed him. Hubert, for fear of some dire misfortune, sent the younger away to St. Petersburg; and he served afterwards as officer under Suwaroff, and fell fighting against the French. Hubert was prevented revealing to the world the dishonest and deceitful way in which he had acquired possession of the estate-tail by the shame and disgrace which would have come upon him; but he would not rob the rightful owner of a single penny more. He caused inquiries to be set on foot in Geneva, and learned that Madame Born had died of grief at the incomprehensible disappearance of her husband, but that young Roderick Born was being brought up by a worthy man who had adopted him. Hubert then caused himself to be introduced under an assumed name as a relative of Born the merchant, who had perished at sea, and he forwarded at given times sufficient sums of money to give the young heir of entail a good and respectable education. How he carefully treasured up the surplus revenues from the estate, and how he drew up the terms of his will, we already know. Respecting his brother's death, Hubert spoke in strangely obscure terms, but they allowed this much to be inferred, that there must be some mystery about it, and that he had taken part, indirectly, at least, in some heinous crime.

The contents of the black portfolio made everything clear. Along with Hubert's traitorous correspondence with Daniel was a sheet of paper written and signed by Daniel. V—— read a confession at which his very soul trembled, appalled. It was at Daniel's instigation that Hubert had come to R— sitten; and it was Daniel again who had written and told him about the one hundred and fifty thousand thalers that had been found. It has been already described how Hubert was received by his brother, and how, deceived in all his hopes and wishes, he was about to go off when he was prevented by V——, Daniel's heart was tortured by an insatiable thirst for vengeance, which he was determined to take on the young man who had proposed to kick him out like a mangy cur. He it was who relentlessly and incessantly fanned the flame of passion by which Hubert's desperate heart was consumed. Whilst in the fir forests hunting wolves, out in the midst of a blinding snowstorm, they agreed to effect his destruction. "Make away with him!" murmured Hubert, looking askance and taking aim with his rifle. "Yes, make away with him," snarled Daniel, "but not in that way, not in that way! " And he made the most solemn asseverations that he would murder the Freiherr and not a soul in the world should be the wiser. When, however, Hubert had got his money, he repented of the plot; he determined to go away in order to shun all further temptation. Daniel himself saddled his horse and brought it out of the stable; but as the Baron was about to mount, Daniel said to him in a sharp, strained voice, "I thought you would stay on the entail, Freiherr Hubert, now that it has just fallen to you, for the proud lord of the entail lies dashed to pieces at the bottom of the ravine, below the tower." The steward had observed that Wolfgang, tormented by his thirst for gold, often used to rise in the night, go to the postern which formerly led to the tower, and stand gazing with longing eyes down into the chasm, where, according to his (Daniel's) testimony, vast treasures lay buried. Relying upon this habit, Daniel waited near the hall-door on that ill-omened night; and as soon as he heard the Freiherr open the postern leading to the tower, he entered the hall and proceeded to where the Freiherr was standing, close by the brink of the chasm. On becoming aware of the presence of his villainous servant, in whose eyes the gleam of murder shone, the Freiherr turned round and said with a cry of terror, "Daniel, Daniel, what are you doing here at this hour?" But then Daniel shrieked wildly, "Down with you, you mangy cur!" and with a powerful push of his foot he hurled the unhappy man over into the deep chasm.

Terribly agitated by this awful deed, Freiherr Roderick found no peace in the castle where his father had been murdered. He went to his Courland estates, and only visited R— sitten once a year, in autumn. Francis — old Francis — who had strong suspicions as to Daniel's guilt, maintained that he often haunted the place at full moon, and described the nature of the apparition much as V—— afterwards experienced it for himself when he exorcised it. It was the disclosure of these circumstances, also, which stamped his father's memory with dishonour, that had driven young

Freiherr Hubert out into the world.

This was my old great-uncle's story. Now he took my hand, and whilst his eyes filled with tears, he said, in a broken voice, "Cousin, cousin! And she too — the beautiful lady — has fallen a victim to the dark destiny, the grim, mysterious power which has established itself in that old ancestral castle. Two days after we left R— sitten the Freiherr arranged an excursion on sledges as the concluding event of the visit. He drove his wife himself; but as they were going down the valley the horses, for some unexplained reason, suddenly taking fright, began to snort and kick and plunge most savagely. 'The old man! The old man is after us!' screamed the Baroness in a shrill, terrified voice. At this same moment the sledge was overturned with a violent jerk, and the Baroness was hurled to a considerable distance. They picked her up lifeless — she was quite dead. The Freiherr is perfectly inconsolable, and has settled down into a state of passivity that will kill him. We shall never go to R— sitten again, cousin!"

Here my uncle paused. As I left him my heart was rent by emotion; and nothing but the all-soothing hand of Time could assuage the deep pain which I feared would cost me my life.

Years passed. V—— was resting in his grave, and I had left my native country. Then I was driven northwards, as far as St. Petersburg, by the devastating war which was sweeping over all Germany. On my return journey, not far from K——, I was driving one dark summer night along the shore of the Baltic, when I perceived in the sky before me a remarkably large bright star. On coming nearer I saw by the red flickering flame that what I had taken for a star must be a large fire, but could not understand how it could be so high up in the air. "Postilion, what fire is that before us yonder?" I asked the man who was driving me. "Oh! why, that's not a fire; it's the beacon tower of R— sitten." "R— sitten!" Directly the postilion mentioned the name all the experiences of the eventful autumn days which I had spent there recurred to my mind with lifelike reality. I saw the Baron — Seraphina — and also the remarkably eccentric old aunts — myself as well, with my bare milk-white face, my hair elegantly curled and powdered, and wearing a delicate sky-blue coat — nay, I saw myself in my love-sick folly, sighing like a furnace, and making lugubrious odes on my mistress's eyebrows. The sombre, melancholy mood into which these memories plunged me was relieved by the bright recollection of V——'s genial jokes, shooting up like flashes of coloured light, and I found them now still more entertaining than they had been so long ago. Thus agitated by pain mingled with much peculiar pleasure, I reached R— sitten early in the morning and got out of the coach in front of the post-house, where it had stopped I recognised the house as that of the land-steward; I inquired after him. "Begging your pardon," said the clerk of the post-house, taking his pipe from his mouth and giving his night-cap a tilt, "begging your pardon; there is no land-steward here; this is a Royal Government office, and the Herr Administrator is still asleep." On making further inquiries I learnt that Freiherr Roderick von R——, the last lord of the entail, had died sixteen years before without descendants, and that the entail in accordance with the terms of the original deeds had now escheated to the state. I went up to the castle; it was a mere heap of ruins. I was informed by an old peasant, who came out of the fir-forest, and with whom I entered into conversation, that a large portion of the stones had been employed in the construction of the beacon-tower. He also could tell the story of the ghost which was said to have haunted the castle, and he affirmed that people often heard unearthly cries and lamentations amongst the stones, especially at full moon.

Poor short-sighted old Roderick! What a malignant destiny did you conjure up to destroy with the breath of poison, in the first moments of its growth, that race which you intended to plant with firm roots to last on till eternity!

Footnotes

1 Freiherr = Baron, though not exactly in the present significance of the term in Germany. A Freiherr belongs to the "superior nobility," and is a Baron of the older nobility of the Middle Ages; and he ranks immediately after a Count (Graf). The title Baron is now restricted to comparatively newer creations, and its bearer belongs to the "lower nobility." In this tale "Freiherr" and "Baron" are used indifferently.

2 The Justitiarius acted as justiciary in the seignorial courts of justice, which were amongst the privileges accorded to the nobility of certain ranks, in certain cases, by the feudal institutions of the Middle Ages. This privilege the R—— family is represented as exercising.

3 At the present time the Germans say Prosit! under like circumstances. This of coarse reminds one of the Greek custom of regarding sneezing as an auspicious omen.

4 This refers to an episode in Schiller's work, related by a Sicilian. The story is of a familiar type. Two brothers, Jeronymo and Lorenzo, fall in love with the same Lady Antonia; the elder brother is secretly killed by the younger. But on the marriage day of the murderer the murdered man appears in the disguise of a monk, and proceeds to reveal himself in his bloody habiliments and show his ghastly wounds.

5 By Paul Fleming (1609–1640); one of the pious but gloomy religious songs of this leading spirit of the "first Silesian school."

7 The reference is to a Landsmannschaft. These were

associations, at a university, of students from the same state or country, bound to the observance of certain traditional customs, &c, and under the control of certain self-elected officers (the Senior being one).

8 Imperial thalers varied in value at different times, but estimating their value at three shillings, the sum here mentioned would be equivalent to about £22,500. A Frederick d'or was a gold coin worth five thalers.